FORGET YOU MUST

REMEMBER

a novel

NATHAN DOUGLAS HANSEN

Jaded Ibis Press

sustainable literature by digital means™

an imprint of Jaded Ibis Productions

Seattle • Hong Kong • Boston

This book is dedicated to the men and women of
America's Armed Forces.

May you have the bravery and courage you need to achieve world
peace, in hopes we will soon take each other up in arms without
taking up arms.

And to Guadalupe, for without I wouldn't have the courage to
speak up.

ONE

The first day doesn't exist, so neither does the bearded man with tired luggage eyes and worn calloused hands taking your blood pressure. Because he doesn't exist, neither does the overweight, overbearing nurse whose shoes sigh puffs of uneasiness and asks if you have suicidal ideations. And because they don't exist, then neither does the assembly line of staff who pass you around a blinding white hallway, a manila folder tabbed orange because the last four digits in your social security number begins with "two." And because that doesn't exist, then perhaps you don't, which for the time being is good, because if you didn't exist, then there wouldn't be a reason for a chain of events that brought you here in the first place. There wouldn't have been a reason for your ex-girlfriend to worry and call your best friend. And if there wasn't that phone call and discussion amplified with tears then your best friend wouldn't have had a reason to visit you at your one-room basement studio in the housing project where rap sheets papered walls that squatters ruled. There'd be no reason for him to push aside a barricade of grocery carts and step over empty liquor bottles, dirty needles and junkies. There'd be no reason for him to knock once, twice, a third time until kicking a rotten door in and finding you unconscious, lying in the fetal position on a cold concrete floor, damp from your own incontinence. And if he wasn't there to stand over you, kneel and note a weak and thready pulse with low respirations, there'd be no reason for that friend to step back outside and call three digits and describe your permanent address and possibly your permanent state of being. There'd be no need to tell a dispatch officer to have an ambulance look for a green trash trailer filled with shingles and siding in the front yard because the number of the building is hidden behind a wall of dead ivy. There would be no need for that friend, calm as this was expected, to excuse the garbage and the busted hallway light and smell of mildew and feces while leading two paramedics to your body where they, too, kneel and begin CPR.[1]

To understand so much about cause and effect, action and reaction, yet want so badly to deny something out of existence is irresponsible. Then again, so is swallowing handfuls of sleeping pills[2] with the intention to let go.[3] Were the pills

---

[1]   1352 This paramedic checked for pulse and breath sounds and upon not finding any began CPR. After one round of 10-2, carotid pulse was found and rescue breathing continued. Pete Kasner, EMT-P, 06/04/09.

[2]   1354 Empty bottle of Donormyl 25 mg found beside victim. Physical evidence lost in transfer. Number of pills victim took is unknown. There were 96 pills per bottle. Pete Kasner, EMT-P, 06/04/09.

[3]   1406 Victim repeatedly stated "let go, let go, let go" during

meant to erase your existence? If so, why deny the existence of this day? Is this a regret—three and a half handfuls of pills in a bottle you should never have had in the first place? Regardless, if this day never existed, you wouldn't have been strapped to a gurney with an oxygen mask**4** hiding your shame and intravenous lines**5** tying you to life. There'd be no reason for that friend, your best friend, to go to the hospital emergency room alone, driving your rusted Ford with two car seats in back, as he promised he would, hoping all the while in a few hours you'll be conscious enough to drive this beloved wreck back home yourself; your devoted friend following flashes of red and an ear-piecing eulogy, the only person you trust enough to pass news of your passing on to family; your best friend, your only family. But out of that friend's hands there is you and your body that may never have made it to the hospital where there'd be no reason for paramedics to cut off your favorite T-shirt—that vintage Led Zeppelin shirt from Walmart— to attach adhesive leads to your bare chest. If it wasn't for them then there wouldn't have been anyone to have found the syncopation between the electronic tone of your heart rate and the ambulance's roar. You wouldn't have been removed from

---

transport. Non-responsive to verbal stimuli. Pete Kasner, EMT-P, 06/04/09.

4   1407 Patient received 75-percent oxygen via full face mask. Pete Kasner, EMT-P, 06/04/09.

5   1412 Patient received 900 ml Ringer's lactate followed by 333ml 5% Dextrose. Pete Kasner, EMT-P, 06/04/09.

the rear of the ambulance like a searing hot pan from the oven, quickly wheeled from a jelly-like fog into a warm light of snow that seemed to melt before it touched your skin. You wouldn't have had liquid charcoal[6] forced upon yourself to absorb the poisoning, once and twice. There wouldn't have been a need for the drawn curtains and ultimate privacy as the urgency settled and I.V. bags[7] were exchanged and a wristband attached. If you denied the day successfully there wouldn't have been the need for a visit from a social worker and a "quick, down and dirty Q and A,"[8] followed by a urinalysis[9] to set at ease any

---

[6]   1414 Liquid charcoal, or Activated carbon, dosing at 1 gram/kg of body weight (for adolescents or adults, give 50-100 g) prescribed first time to bind on toxin and prevent stomach and intestinal absorption. Second application prescribed by presiding emergency room physician Dr. Charles Noel to interrupt enterohepatic circulation. Discontinued after second application. Margaret Kyle, RN, 06/04/09.

[7]   1417 Patient received 1000 ml 0.9% NaCl on moderate drip. Margaret Kyle, RN, 06/04/09.

[8]   1515 Patient is relatively unresponsive despite efforts to create a background chart. Refused to answer name and address as well as date, including day, month, year. Diane Cowell, LCSW, 06/04/09.

[9]   1522 Urinalysis ordered per Christine Huot, RN, 06/04/09.

Urine Collection "Clean Catch" Method for Males:
- Wash your hands thoroughly.
- Draw foreskin back away from the urinary opening.
- Open the towelette and wipe the urinary opening and the surrounding area. Discard the towelette in the wastebasket.
- Begin to urinate into the toilet. Wait until the urine stream is well established and move the empty container into the path of the stream. Catch the middle portion of your flow.
- Screw the cap onto the container securely without touching the inside rim.

question that your tendencies might be drug-driven, and a psychiatric evaluation**10** where the same questions echoed in whispers behind the nurses' station and answers lingered on your tongue. There wouldn't have been a need for insurance paperwork and promissory notes to repay people who did what you didn't want and kept you alive, a promise requiring initials and signatures of your full name, middle included. Hours later, if this day didn't happen and you didn't exist there wouldn't have been the need for the embarrassing escort by security past an information booth manned with elderly volunteers through a *hush* of automatic doors into a bleak fall evening and barren parking lot. You wouldn't have had to stand like a poster child of fragile mortality beneath EMERGENCY in red neon towered by a neon blue cross so similar to your signature. There wouldn't have been the need for a van with government license plates to pick you up curbside and transport you—the living dead and hideous self-proclaimed victim of circumstances—directly to a facility for the mentally unsound, a skeleton of trash.

And, completing the circle, if you didn't exist, which you do, you wouldn't now sit before the bearded man with tired

---

- Make sure the container is labeled correctly.
- Return urine sample to the lab.
- If you have any questions, please ask laboratory employee.

10   1511 25-year-old Caucasian male admitted ambulatory without a gait problem and is not a fall risk. Comes in with complaints of paranoia and suicidal ideation, contracts for safety. Denies any pain. No known amount of money, did not declare. Well-oriented to time, place and person. Weight stable at 165 lbs. Claims allergy to penicillin that causes rash and difficulty. William Balding, Psy.D., 06/04/09.

luggage eyes who has seen more than you're willing to risk and handled more than you're willing to weigh. You would never hear the breathless words of the nurse whose walk sighs anguish. And you would never begin yet another life inside a manila folder, tabbed orange, passed hand to hand, desk to desk. Hindsight, your existence seems a digression and you'll forever wonder if there's a beginning to it all.

TWO

"Hey, son, could you please roll up your sleeve?"

You hear him. You open your eyes, and a figure in white sits on a wheeled stool before you, on a sea-foam green bed lined with white paper. He is right in front of you seated as you are, but mobile, sliding his stool to and fro with a slight push from his toes. His broad coarse mustache is a curtain hiding his words like nurses' whispers. His leathered face tells tales as dark and haggard as his complexion, and a lingering pipe smell flows from his every twist, turn and slide. Place him behind a podium in a tweed jacket and wool scarf and he's a tenured professor spouting a dense intellect, but deeper down you know the most he has ever written, let alone contemplated or researched, are the checkmarks and numerals on patients' health physicals he is charged with filling out for every late night arrival—blood pressure, pulse, temperature, height, weight, oxygen saturation. Nearly all of this work is done by a portable machine that is pushed and pulled around the ER. But despite the ever-changing world and dependency on automation, humans still need to document. The world needs

Homo sapiens senses to gather knowledge and the articulation to pass it on.

"Son, here, let me help you."

His hands peel your skin back. You want to howl but your head is cotton and your mouth paste. You blink with your respirations—close and exhale, open and inhale. Exhaling, you imagine yourself outdoors hugging a cottonwood tree. The man's hands are bark running the length of your arms. You picture the tree's canopy extending skyward and inversely the roots burying themselves deeper. The tree, despite its coarse texture, gives and receives, exhales and inhales. The tree is gone and you see people in a lobby you recognize as the Hayward Charles Veterans Affairs Hospital in Phoenix, Arizona. You're in an emergency waiting room. No, different? There's a slower pace, a lack of urgency here. People, the employed and the unable, shuffle as if burdened with apathy. Everyone is sick— dying to get in, dying to get out. People talk over one another or to no one at all. The man reappears as a vision before you. Real? Yes, too real. Inhaling, you watch him scan from wrist to elbow. You want to tell him you are not a drug addict, there's no need to look for track marks, but that may not necessarily be the case. If memory serves you right there was a bottle of pills, and, if truth be told, a knife. You build the courage to look beyond the man's rough exterior only to see a face frozen in malcontent: mouth pursed and shifting under a salt and pepper shade as if siphoning truth. Rusting eyes leak sap into crusted corners visible through bifocals that rest on the bridge of his nose peering and transfixed on your dilated pupils blinded behind welled-up tears. You close your eyes to prevent a single drop from falling only to feel his branches lift the dead weight of your left hand up and through a vinyl cuff. Buttons are pushed and a pump sounds. Slowly, the cuff inflates and tightens, and you think of grade school when your sixth-grade teacher Mr. Stevens led you by the arm to the gymnasium where he asked you if you wanted to be a man. You can still smell his hot black coffee breath in the profanity he whispered—breath much the same as the tired man beside you but in a kinder, gentler tone.

"All right, now this machine is going to take your vital signs,"[11] caffeine says.

You hear the word "vital" and stem on its importance. You want to know how the machine knows what is vital. You want to ask the weary man what signs are factors for vitality. You remain silent, breathing open and closed, the sterile landscape of an oppressive room and building growing brighter and brighter with the night.

"You'll feel a little pressure on your arm, but it's just the machine measuring your blood pressure."

You smell his voice. Black coffee. No sugar. No cream. His words are as rough as his hands fumbling for something tangible to grasp, contradicting what you expect to be disregard.

"It might be tight for a second but it has to get a pretty good grip in order to get an accurate measure."

---

[11]   1701 Patient's blood pressure is 90/60, borderline hypotensive. Patient's heart rate is 68 b.p.m. Based on physicals two years prior, this is normal. Patient's O2 Sat. is 97. Patient's temperature is 99.2. Maxwell Driscoll, LPN 06/04/09.

You inhale and see a silver name badge: Max.

"This thing will measure your pulse, your heart rate. And this plastic clip I put on the end of your finger measures your O2 sat... That means it measures your oxygen saturation," he says. "That's medical jargon for the percentage of oxygen in your blood."

With all the medical gadgetry taking the place of people, you know Max's job is on the line like you know your life is. There's no use for you anymore. You blink tearful eyelashes.

"Let me check out your eyes,"**12** the bag man says. "You feeling pretty down, huh? Wanna hurt yourself? Don't worry 'bout this, son. They're just gonna get you checked in, then you can't get some rest."

And with that, you are grabbed under the arm and stood up.

"This day doesn't even exist," Max says. "This day you have to forget, yet never let out of your memory. Understand?"

---

12   1703 Patient's pupils are equal and reactive to light and accommodation—PERLA. Maxwell Driscoll, LPN, 06/04/09.

THREE

You're baggage, led physically, lugged mentally, down a hallway illuminated as bright as sunbeams on the night's fallen snow. Pillars from heaven run floor to ceiling as the fluorescent lights lead you infinitely nowhere, reflecting your figure off a floor's freshly laid wax, the opaque glass of closed office doors and the first floor windows of Hayward Charles' Psychiatric Admissions—for a moment the Holy Trinity. You shuffle your feet to God, and will stride out when you begin to accept him. You don't, and instead accept the evening's fate—the first step, if sanity could be quantified as such. You estimate it will be a long journey to the next destination because your handler brings his coffee mug. In his opposite hand, cared for as gently as the steaming scalding drink, is your medical file. The manila folder is light enough—it, too, reflects the hallway's illumination. You watch it flow back and forth under the grasp of the man's fingertips. You imagine it is the death certificate of your soul seeking a final set of signatures. "Who's next?" you say under your breath.

"I'm taking you to the charge nurse, then onto a social

worker," Max says. "She's going to start the intake proceedings."
You wonder if he heard you. Did he read your mind?

FOUR

Max corrals you into an office an entire hallway down from the lobby where he took your first set of vitals. As he turns you inside and guides you to a plastic, tongue-shaped chair, his grip tightens as if to brace you for something unexpected. When you look to him in response to the pain you see a face appear from the hall and slide between you and him. All faces seem to look the same anymore, but this one is new and kneels before you. Blonde hair in a pony tail, she wears a white T-shirt under black scrubs. She wears no make-up, except black eyeliner that thickens small lashes batting over green eyes. Thin lips are pink flowers leafed open in the middle complimenting rosy cherub cheeks. Her innocence intrudes and suffocates. She introduces herself as "Annie" (though her nametag reads "Lee Anne") then asks you to blow into a breathalyzer. You trust. You tell her you don't drink and she nods, her ponytail bouncing gingerly up and down, side-to-side.

"Of course, it's just precaution," she says. "Standard operating procedure."

She holds a tube up to your mouth and you blow.[13] She reads the digital monitor and asks you to do it once again.

"Harder this time," she says.

You blow and she walks off satisfied with the zero reading. You tell her she should have believed you but she only smiles. She returns with a hypodermic needle and three empty vials, and bends over you, running her fingers along the inside of the arm that was suspected of being induced with intravenous drugs moments ago. Trust goes both ways, so you've been told.

"Yeah, well, now I have to draw some blood. Again, S.O.P."

You watch her index finger rub the inside of your elbow and find a plump bloodline. You hear her tell coffee to hand her three "red top" vials for a blood draw.[14]

"Please," she says.

Her hair smells of lilacs and a berry you cannot recognize, and she's close enough you can tell the T-shirt she's wearing doesn't belong to her. It's a man's T-shirt—her boyfriend's that she's borrowed. You overhear her telling fellow nurses about last night's sexual escapades and how she woke up late this morning and hurriedly got dressed for work at her boyfriend's

---

[13] 1755 Breathalyzer reading: 0.0, per Lee Anne FitzSimmons, RN, 06/04/09

[14] 1759 Per telephonic order with Grant Michaels, MD: obtain CBC (complete blood count), BMP (basic metabolic panel) TSH (tests thyroid function) and toxicology (drug and alcohol content). Lee Anne FitzSimmons, 06/04/09.

apartment. She forgot an undershirt so grabbed one of his, so now she can still smell him and it's driving her crazy. You imagine her back at her boyfriend's—better yet, back at your place. She's dressed, fresh from a shower, in the kitchen having breakfast in nothing but her panties, bra (Victoria's Secret, soft pink) and your T-shirt. Her legs are smooth and shaven and shining in the morning light. Beneath it all, you want to meet your mouth to her breasts and feel her nipples harden under the weight of your tongue, but you know there exists a feeling of malaise from her toward your kind, a group you have experienced as a member in a society unmindful of the mindless. You know what it is to be a part of the misunderstood minority, a veteran, and refugee in one's own country. You've seen veterans fill this hospital daily, a hospital no different than the half dozen you've spent weeks and months in. You've seen nurses the same type, a candy-coated shell of consideration filled with a growing resentment for routine and coerced by words such as "Duty," "Honor," "Selfless Service," and "Personal Courage." These are the same words the Armed Forces used on your friends, the Army specifically on you, and perhaps Annie too. Like the recycled air tasting stale after it's pumped through vents and ducts, you are a stagnant, torn piece of a giant puzzle that a system has long since given up on. Where do you lie? Where does Annie? Her touch is soft and sensual and gives you goose pimples.

"Cold?" she asks.

No, you tell her. You tell her it feels good. You tell her that her touch seems to thaw this numb body, then you hear a calculated guffaw of a man, and you smell the coffee breath.

She lowers her head more, and all but her ear and the corners of her eye and mouth can be seen. She bats her lashes. Does she smile? You can't tell. Your arm is swabbed with alcohol and a tourniquet wrapped around your bicep. You stare down at her shoes—Nike with a pink swoosh to match her pink stethoscope. The image of her standing half-naked with you in her mouth ends with you wincing at a needle prick and a question lingering in the air about an "available bed to fill." She makes a call from a nearby phone and you estimate she must be relatively new. She is fresh, enthusiastic, and productive. She has yet to become jaded.

"Yes? The only bed available? I want it," she says, and lowers her voice into anonymity while marking off your chart. **15**

---

15   1823 Per Lee Anne FitzSimmons, RN, 06/04/09.

FALL RISK ASSESSMENT SCALE INTERVENTIONS—a score > = to 45 (identifies 70% of fallers) interventions:

X—Place bed in low position

X—Wear non-slip footwear when ambulating

X—Orient to unit and surroundings (bathroom, call light, etc.)

X—Patient education

FIVE

You heave yourself listlessly from the mouth of your station back into the hall. Tips of fingers from a free hand push you down this pine-scented thoroughfare to yet another toll booth—a place to exhibit your difference, your change. You're checked into a cubicle where another person in white awaits. This person is a woman, black as the coffee smell lingering on the tired man's breath. She is naturally obese, large in a way that suits her so she couldn't be pictured as any other form: big breasts weighing down broad shoulders balancing a double chin of frowns all supported beneath a waist wider than the arms of the chair that holds her. She has a clipboard on her lap and more medical sheets—a questionnaire. Before the baggage handler leaves you ask if this day truly exists, but he doesn't respond and instead walks off to another series of blood pressures, pulses, oxygen saturation counts, height and weight measurements. Someone else will listen to his coffee breath and drink up his compassion, watch him push his wheeled stool to and fro.

You settle slowly, like dust, in another chair in the cubicle shared with the woman. The question you asked the man is written on a separate line of a separate page in the same orange-tabbed folder of checkmarks and initials. You watch the woman writing. You secretly name her Jules. You name her Jules after Julie Pucette, the first girlfriend who encountered the real you. You met Julie in Kansas where you were a flight medic with the U.S. Army nearly a decade prior. She was attending Kansas State University and majoring in Engineering, and regardless of her sour sense of humor and family-fed ego, you believed you were in love and eloped weeks after knowing her. You knew the military would pay you more money with dependents, and the increase of salary sounded good to both Julie and you. Julie would pay her rent and you would do whatever came to your mind at the moment.

Julie was bright and beautiful, like a diamond, thus "Jewels" or as you preferred spelling it, J-U-L-E-S. On the contrary, her world revolved around her classes and textbooks and a sorority, in which she was determined to get accepted. When you were admitted to the hospital in Kansas, reciting sermons spoken to you by invisible people and believing you were a descendent of Christ, she listened to doctors' explanations for brain chemistry, not to mention advice to remain supportive, but she stayed away, fearful. She learned about manic-depression and psychotic symptoms but never shared the information. She bought a couple books but never cracked the table of contents. She came to visit only once, which happened to be the time you consummated your marriage in her Chevy Camaro outside the Veterans Administrative Hospital in Topeka—a marriage of three weeks followed by a $500 annulment and fallacy of love. Now a new Jules is in your life and she mouths your words as she inscribes, "Doesn't...even...exist." You hear her pen rake the paper.**16** You hear her breathing heavy through the words, exhaling through her nose to hide the obvious respiratory distress suffered from obesity. You don't care. You know you'd watch her die if she were to collapse in front of you, Jules the heavy black woman documenting your uncertainty. At the moment you wish she'd let you die. You'd let her watch. She shifts her legs, as little as she can move them, and you hear her shoes exhale and inhale, the same as your eyes fighting to take it all in and stay alive.

"Okay, what brings you in here this evening?" she asks.

She mentions no name. You aren't a name, you're a number, a statistic. Names don't matter here. You are not sure what matters, so you question what you have yet to decide: if reality matters.

Do the bodiless footsteps you hear encroaching upon you count as reality?

Is it real if there is nobody to walk in accompaniment of

---

16   1936 HISTORY OF PRESENT ILLNESS: History of present illness is at this point sporadic due to patient's extreme paranoia and lack of collaborating information from outside sources. Patient is extremely tearful, very labile during the interview. He is extraordinarily paranoid and states he does not wish to discuss what has been going on recently again. He states he has a great deal of trust problems, that he has had difficulties with thinking since childhood. He states that he feels tired of "playing the game" and believes that every time he trusts someone they go away and he has to start over. Melinda Hanner, LCSW, 06/04/09.

those sounds?

Does it matter that they haunt you?

Does it matter you include the man, dressed in black and always to your left, when making headcounts?

If he doesn't exist does it matter?

You named him Walter Dunn and he is as alive as you.**17**

And what about the white light, that light that burns you feverishly from behind your eyes and swallows you whole?

Does it matter that it is only you who can see and feel this light as if you stood alone in the middle of a freeway arms outstretched to embrace the destructive impact of a semi-tractor trailer at 120 miles per hour?

Does it matter you hear your name called as whispers and you blame all those around you for their cruel deception?

What brings you here?

It rings in your head and you wonder if it matters.

Truth is subjective. Your truth is different from their truth, and all the while you feel you are living a lie. Ironically, the

---

17   2007 Resident Gisick's speech is tangential and difficult to follow. He is paranoid that the CIA (which is in actuality trying to hire him due to his knowledge of Arabic) is monitoring his every move. He exhibits some grandiosity, stating that he has knowledge that average people don't have and it is frustrating for him to try to explain these things to them because they can't understand (e.g., that there were actually 20 planes hijacked on 9/11/01, including planes in Korea and Alaska, but the US Government was able to thwart those hijacking in some unspecified way). Currently, he denies any changes in sleep or appetite, but he does state that in the past he has stayed up all night, writing furiously his ideas for plays, novels, short stories, etc. Melinda Hanner, LCSW, 06/04/09

more honestly you live, the more you feel used and deceived and they call it paranoia. Who are "they"? They are the people you have to learn to trust.

"Do you feel like hurting yourself, sir? Sir?"

The woman's cubicle walls are enshrined with photographs of young adults and grandchildren; framed, pin-holed, taped and held by magnets, an entourage of two-dimensional family members all posed—no candids. No picture of any men. No wedding ring. You wonder if she'd have sex with you. You wonder if she could get your flaccid penis hard. If she were married you wonder if she'd even care.

"Are we having a tough time, or what?" she asks.

A menagerie of Beanie Babies graze among the paperwork scattered around Jules' desk—this is her life. You know why there are no pictures of men and no wedding ring.

"Are we having a tough time, *or what*?"

She leans towards you, her head cocked sideways. The closer she gets and the more she turns her head the louder her voice, as if proximity and rotation of her head control her volume. Jules hasn't slept in two days and you see it in the red cracks shooting from behind the eggshell whites of her eyes. Almond-colored concealer hides insomnia, blending smoothly and deceptively with light rouge on her cheeks making her dark skin mocha. She leans so close you can smell her cocoa butter skin lotion and feel each word pass by your earlobes. She sighs in frustration and sits upright once again, a low tide after crashes of unanswered waves.

"Sir, have you been thinking about hurting yourself?" Jules

asks. "Have you thought about hurting others?"

You sit, buckled into a rollercoaster in a theme park of intermittent conversations and sounds: a receptionist paging the Charge Nurse, keeping her boyfriend waiting on the other line; a doctor discussing with a colleague what will make the Harley-Davidson Fat Boy a classic; the sudden squeak of white soft leather shoes with non-marking soles sprinting towards a stainless steel surgical tray's metallic crash and sobering wail of a patient in withdrawal; the pneumatic *whoosh* of double-doors opening automatically and a gurney's wheels rolling hymn of crumpled sandpaper; another doctor agreeing the Harley would forever be a classic, but he will never give up riding his dual-sport motorcycle, nor will he quit driving his Porsche 911 or fully restored 1956 Chevy Bel-Air; a dialogue of clicking pen tops, ballpoint drum rolls and the low baritone of Jules' anxious hum ready to ask more questions on how you received tickets for this ride.

"I guess I'll take that as a 'yes,'" she says.

What was the question, you ask. She looks up from the medical file, removes the ballpoint pen from her mouth, a blue cap chewed flat shines wet in the fluorescent lights. The glisten resembles the barrel of a 12-gauge shotgun you once rested in your mouth sitting in a bedroom of a house you shared with an ex-fiancé in North Carolina. You couldn't pull the trigger then, like you couldn't pull it living in Iowa or California, because you didn't want a loved one to have to see what you imagined would be a horrific sight. Who cleaned up self-inflicted scenes such as these, you asked yourself then and still ask to this day. Jules writes, and the scratching of quick strikes and strokes synchronizes with the harmonious sounds outside the cubicle.[18] The waving of the pen is a conductor's wand, the intake an orchestra. You hear less and less as more and more questions arise. You try to lift your eyebrows to open your eyes, only to lean your head back, forehead wrinkled and blind. Everything is connected to something else and nothing works. Then begins that conversation, that voice nobody hears but you—the one-sided debate with self, the one reason for the hospitalization.

Hey. Hey. Here.

What? What was that? Did you just call my name again?

You understand, don't you?

Where are you?

Here. No, over here. Behind you. To your left, in the slightest peripheral—at your right if cornered—looking sharp wearing a black suit; black shoes; black tie; white shirt; cufflinks of silver, platinum maybe.

What's going on?

---

[18] 1954 PSYCHOSOCIAL HISTORY: Patient reports that he grew up in Lonas, Iowa. He lived there with his mother and father and one older sister. He reports his sister is nine years older than he is and that his mother had nine miscarriages before giving birth to him, in turn making him a "miracle child." He reports being close to his family. His father works at a sporting goods store, his mother is a teacher and dance instructor. He is currently married and has been for the past three weeks, although he doesn't live with his wife and married her "for the fun of it." He states this is his second marriage. He has two children—a six-year-old and a two-year-old. He was married once before and was divorced sometime in 2004. Melinda Hanner, LCSW, 06/04/09.

What's wrong?

You're used to hearing the ticking, the tocking, that perpetual clock sound. You're used to the seconds running a horse's gallop, steady, the Pony Express skipping that special delivery to you. Yesterday, those seconds were clicking railroad tracks and today, worse, the sound is a march under Hitler's salute. Time imprisons you.

Here...here...here.

The scraping sounds you hear could be that missing set of scissors hovering outside the basement window you blacked out with boot wax and a Sharpie. It could be the transmitter the military placed in your eardrum, hearing what you hear, what you say, what you think. It could be your imagination. Then again, you're rather intelligent, right?

What do you want, you plea.

Me, or the shadow that paces outside your hovel door? Don't take the razor you shave with and place it to your wrist, it won't cut deep enough. It won't cut deep enough to sever tendons like I imagine you'd want to do. And don't take any pills, or am I too late?

Your body wants to erupt, shed its skin. You stand and scream that the world will leave you alone. You didn't do it. You didn't do it.

Jules' chair flies back and you hear it bang against her desk. Her voice booms, head cocked? You aren't sure.

"Doctor, this guy's losing it," she says, waving your file over the cubicle wall.

Your shoulders are pushed back against the wall of the

cubicle. A magnet falls onto the desk, nearly decapitating a Beanie Baby. The voice of the Harley-Davidson fan buries into you then a stainless steel needle.[19] He says something slow and methodical as his thumb drops the plunger and injects a chemically-based sleep, leaving you with Jules' graying face eclipsing a fluorescent sun. You want to tell this doctor you once owned a Harley and that you paid for it outright with cash, but you question the story's validity. You want to tell him you did have a Harley and once drove it up the Pacific Coast Highway from Los Angeles to Monterey, but you don't know if you've really been there. You don't know where you've ever been or where you are now. You feel yourself caving, folding into yourself, and then you hear something you hope will define you and what is happening. "Ward 5-C, Ward 5-C" an overhead loudspeaker says, sullen and monotone. The surgical tray's fall crescendos, a gurney's vibrato falls off down a distant hallway, ballpoint snares slip back into pockets and drawers and Charge Nurse calls for an intermission. Discussions on the howling pipes of a 1974 Panhead continue while the curtains of the elevator proscenium leading to Act Five, Ward 5, Ward 5-C, swallows you whole with two sets of hands pinching you behind the elbows and guiding you forward then turning you 180 degrees.

"Say 'goodbye,'" a man on your left elbow says.

"And get ready to say, 'Hello,'" right elbow finishes.

---

[19] 2002 100 mg of Thorazine administered IM for mania. Grant Michaels, MD, 06/04/09.

31

SIX

Hello. You've said "hello" before. You greeted Cherokee Mental Health Institute in Iowa when you were a juvenile pending charges on aggravated assault. Friends who saw you pull a knife on an upperclassman knew you were only trying to scare him, but parents of the boy thought otherwise. They believed their son's story over yours, as did a judge. You courted staff during hundreds of hours spent in outpatient care while in high school followed by college, during both undergraduate and graduate studies. You remember the stone face exteriors of courthouses, as cold and quiet as a cathedral, only less forgiving. You remember placing your hand on leather-bound Holy Bibles while being sworn in by a bailiff and looking over rows of mahogany benches, the judge beside you presiding as a minister before a curious congregation filling this church's pews. You remember being preached Freud and Jung and common sense and self-esteem. You remember your mother asking about the half-dozen concussions you experienced trying to be heroic during junior high football and whether or not they might have a say in your condition. You remember the military—a novel life with too many chapters—and discharge orders, passed on from Veterans Hospitals in Topeka to Fayetteville, North Carolina, to Los Angeles, now to Phoenix—you are to rise from the ashes in Phoenix. You remember swallowing tubes. You remember wrist-bound bandages. Scars are more than a memory. Scars are proof medical staff see and judge your legitimacy. How far will you go? Nobody likes an unblemished victim. You are a prisoner of your own mind and everything has say but you.

"Going up," the man on your left says.

The elevator buckles your knees as it begins its ascent. You are held by your puppeteers, hanging with too many strings attached. You close your eyes and imagine Saint Peter greeting you, but you still feel your feet touching the elevator floor and know a true ascension to heaven would be weightless, brighter, dignified. There would be harps instead of ballads. You hear laughter, and for a moment you think maybe it is you accepting this fate—but deep down you've accepted nothing more than the sterile judgment of a few people who are preliminary steps down a long road, not of recovery or rehabilitation. The laughter isn't yours for you haven't the energy to lift your jowls to smile. It is your puppeteers' chuckling, dangling your body into a swaying rhythm in time with their shaking heads. They laugh in disbelief, Russian dolls, towering, no-necked and broad, hiding what little soul they have hollowed out inside shallow molds layered over one another.

"Second floor, hardware and appliances," the man on your right says. "Third floor, entertainment: stereos, televisions, camcorders, DVD players. Fourth floor, ladies lingerie, and fifth floor, children's toys . . . "

"Puréed food, puzzles and babysitting," says the man on your left.

These brute men geared with batons, tazers and mace sound off with muffled insult, warps of leather belts and dishonesty and a stench of sharp cologne. The lift is an eternity and when the elevator jerks to a stop you're jerked too, no longer sagging and lifeless but upright and less a life. Voices clear and huffs of breath are exhaled through nasal passages. Sarcasm opens drawn curtains and no audience is to be found. You are led three steps into the hallway, pulled and pushed, a young puppy fighting obedience. You lift your head in despair, the tendons in your neck sore from its bobbing and nodding. The right puppetmaster pushes a button below a speaker on the wall. The transmission sounds like a snoring television station asleep after the National Anthem.

"Hello. We have another body for you."

Another body, not somebody.

SEVEN

The first person to greet you at the magnetically charged double doors of ward 5-C is Eunice, a nurse's assistant. Eunice hails from Nigeria and her accent is as thick and dark and beautiful as her skin. Slow and methodical she checks your vital signs a second time for the evening. You resign to her mired handiwork as she takes your arm and places it in an inflatable cuff and puts a thermometer in your mouth.[20] As pressure grips your arm yet another time, giant turquoise rings handcrafted by the Navajo roll side-to-side on small fingers forcing her to wiggle them in place as if playing a concerto in air. Stones the color of Arizona skies are mismatched against jewelry passed down generations, African and Indian cultures combine and clash.

---

[20] 2033 Temp is 98.1, BP is 136/84. Eunice Binoli, LPN, 06/04/09

EIGHT

You always wished for large hands. By definition, large hands meant nothing, but the implications behind them suggested a boy was a man. With large hands you could throw a better spiral and palm a basketball, and it was assumed you were well-endowed, but the reason you wished for large hands was to cradle someone in need as much as you wanted to be the one held.

Brian Reynolds had large hands, but he was also a person one psychologist insisted was a "liability" and "underlying contributor" to the deterioration of your mental condition. He hurt you, yet you looked up to him as the guy who stood up to all the bullies in the neighborhood and was practically a brother. You grew up in a small town in Iowa, but it didn't mean you didn't have your share of hurt. In some respects, hurt is greater in a less dense community since a village environment promises to be one to foster growth and not hinder. In a sense, small-town living produces big problems, so big people can't see them right in front of their eyes. Brian was seven years older than you, and during his years in high school he wasn't only the town's All-American boy (straight-A student participating in all sports and extra-curricular activities), he was your own private hero. His parents and yours were friends, and you can recall on certain occasions going to their house with your folks during weekend afternoons to have coffee or tea. You sat around with a glass of tea you sweetened with snuck tablespoons of sugar and listened to grown-up talk for a short while until sneaking into Brian's room to look at his belongings: posters of National Football League quarterbacks, a bookshelf filled with encyclopedias, model airplanes hanging from the ceiling, and trophies in everything from little league to spelling bees. Sometimes you found Brian's class ring on his dresser. It was heavy gold with as many symbols for the activities he participated in inscribed on the sides: football, basketball, track, baseball, choir, student council, math and chess clubs. The center stone was topaz, beautifully shined and sparkling. You never bought a class ring so you always wondered if the center stone was for one's birth month or if they just chose a stone. Why did he choose topaz? You tried the ring on each time you found it, but the only finger it fit was your thumb. Even then you held your hand out as if it were a gift bestowed on you by royalty. With your arms stretched out all you could see was the tip of your thumbnail. You remember Brian wearing this ring and mentioning to his parents and yours dreams of being accepted into the United States Air Force Academy. He wanted to fly. His hands wrote these conversations in the air forcefully as he demanded his need to fly. Secretly you wanted him to, also. So secretly that you never let anyone know how much you cared for him, the young man you wished was your brother, someone to protect solely you. You kept this secret by never letting anyone know you had interest in him, never letting anyone know you entered his room. Even as a child you knew to wipe away wet rings of condensation the glass of tea left on the bureau, and you backed out of his room, combing the footprints out of the shag carpeting. This wasn't your only secret.

NINE

Eunice's smile melts away as she reads numbers you anticipate: low blood pressure, low pulse, no fever. You know your body but not well enough to stay well, to stay out of the hospital. She says you are healthy. She uses the word "healthy" and you can't help but shake your head. Healthy isn't choosing promiscuous sex over family and spending IRAs on bar tabs. Healthy isn't answering to voices others don't hear summoning you. Healthy isn't pondering ways to dispose of your own corpse after suicide to save your friends and family the mess, the clean up or the effort.

After vitals are logged, Eunice takes inventory of your belongings and asks you to change from your street clothes into a pair of pajamas, the patient's daily uniform on the ward. You stand in the cold empty hallway shivering in your boxers hugging yourself for warmth, listening to Eunice's drumming dialect echo the empty hall as she grabs each jeans pocket on the outside before pulling the lining inside-out.

"Do you have any weapon?"

"No brass, no ammo, Drill Sergeant," you say.

"What?"

"Nothing."

It's been hours since the paramedics brought you to a hospital. It's been hours after that that you've sat in sterilized lobbies waiting your turn to be seen. Since then you have woken a bit, enough to make small comments in hopes that you aren't judged by sympathy. You've always pictured yourself as one to make people happy, make them laugh. Your efforts so early into an admission are in vain.

"No, what you say?" Eunice's sentence is mono-syllabic and full of bass, angry.

"I was making a reference to boot camp, when drill sergeants did searches of our belongings after being on the firing line. It didn't mean anything. I was trying to... Never mind."

"Oh, no... You never mind. I'm no drill sergeant. I'm being safe," she says, vengeful. "I don't know you. Do I? I am safe."

"Do you have any weapon?"

"No."

"Do you have any cigarettes?"

"I don't smoke."

"Do you have a cell phone?"

"Yeah, it's in one of my pockets. Somewhere." Your hands feel how much weight you've lost in the past month—twig thighs beneath a doughy middle. Each hand rubs its opposite arm, thin. Fifteen, twenty pounds. There have been mixed reactions from everyone who is close enough to know you, and among the people you know, you trust everyone differently. Some compliments may be insults, whereas some insults may come as compliments.

"What *size* are you?" Eunice says, drawing out the long vowels.

"Excuse me?"

"Size. What *size* are you?"

She raises her voice agitated by the request for clarity. All the while she keeps her eyes on task, searching for contraband blankly as you stare at a growing pile of personal effects that are the only things defining the sane side of your life.

"I don't know wha—"

"Size! Small, medium or large."

"Oh, size! Medium, medium please."

Eunice takes your belongings and places them into a clear plastic bag and zip-ties it secure. She writes your last name and last four digits of your social security number on it in black bold marker—GISICK 2938. The bag is then placed in the nurses' station where someone from Patient Property and Belongings will retrieve it and lock it in a hospital safe. She tosses you a bundle of green clothing, tops and bottoms. They look like an inexpensive version of doctor or nurse's scrubs, something you'd see in a low budget film or soap opera.

"Do you feel like hurting yourself?" Eunice asks.

She watches for your lips to move then gauges your head and whether it will shake or nod. You do nothing. It is barely enough to remain standing half-dressed slipping your legs through hospital pants and snapping two, three buttons.

"Do you feel like hurting others?"

She turns away from you despite catching you vulnerable,

marking what you believe to be your answers onto a white sheet of paper attached to a clip board. Over her shoulder she glimpses and sees you fully dressed, sliding your feet into blue socks with rubberized soles. Again, you say nothing, do nothing. How she will interpret you, you can only imagine.

"Are you hearing things? Seeing things?"

You nod.

"What?" she asks.

"You, right now." Another poor attempt to lighten the mood.

"Fine. What is your level of pain, one being 'very little' and ten being 'extreme pain.'"

"Eight," you say. "I have a horrible headache."

You are dehydrated. You wonder how many tears one must cry to die.

Eunice is monotone in speech and action, bland. A bright yellow shirt contradicts her soul and when unbuttoned suggests she is flirtatious, perhaps willing. Her affect dims your level of arousal and you instead examine her as she writes something down then hands you a sheet of paper listing all the items on inventory: jeans, shirt, undershirt, socks, license, credit card, cell phone. There are no notes on your condition, and you wonder what the purpose of asking questions was. She asks you to sign to ensure those are the only belongings you have. There is no lift in her voice, no intonation. In response, you sign an "X" in blue ink.

Eunice catches how fast you write your name and takes the paper away from you shyly. "Okay, Mr. X, now you wait for the nurse. She will give you something for pain."

TEN

The top half of a door across the hall opens and an emaciated older man pops his head out.

"Gisick—2938?" he says.

You respond by walking up to the door and allowing him to scan your bracelet—proof that you are who you claim to be.

"I'm the night's pharmacy technician," he says. "Here's some pain medication.[21]"

You ask what it is and he repeats his last two words.

"Pain medication."

A giant pink tablet rests in a tiny white cup. A Dixie cup of water is filled and set beside it. You throw the pill in your mouth and swallow it down with a gulp of the cold water. You crumple both cups and throw them in the trashcan beside the pharmacy technician.

"So, does it mean the higher the number I give you, the higher the dosage of medication?" you ask.

"It means good night, Mr. Gisick."

---

[21]   2052 800 milligrams of Ibuprofen ordered for pain. Jack Fletcher, Pharm. Tech., 06/04/09.

ELEVEN

Her name is Tasha and she is the night's charge nurse, your nurse. She's a petite black woman wearing an unflattering emerald velour ensemble, a stay-at-home tracksuit. She smiles wide, walking pigeon-toed as she leads you into a dark room with a line of windows bedazzled with lights from the outside world.

"Million-dollar view," she says. "Yes sir, million-dollar view. People would pay a million dollars for this view."

You feel as if you'd plummet a thousand feet into an abyss if you were to walk up to the window. Unsure and unstable, you stand in the middle of the room, and she points to one of four beds and tells you this is where you will sleep. How long? You ask. All Tasha can tell you is that you'll be here until you're feeling better. You have a feeling that you're not the one who dictates whether or not you feel better. You feel you will have to learn to trust someone else with that judgment. Again, trust. Who will be this someone?

Tasha tells you more about the view. Coyote Butte, Miner's Bluff, and Fire Mountain can all be seen from the window closest to your bed. At the other side, she says, you can see the entire east side of Phoenix into the Painted Desert and New Mexico. You don't disagree, but Tasha's geography is as bad as her choice of clothing. You understand she's trying to make you feel comfortable and she makes up for everything with her pleasantries, especially after Eunice's ghost of an introduction.

"In the morning you can see forever," she says. "I don't actually know for sure because I work the swing shift, nights, but the staff on the graveyard shift says the sun reflects off the desert into pastel colors. Sam, she's a nurse, she says it looks like a painting. Monet or Manet, or something like that. I think she's an artist. What is it you do?"

No matter how you answer her question it doesn't matter; you are wearing green pajamas with a Veteran's Administration logo imprinted on both the top left pocket and pants bottom. You are a model of psychiatric care. And as a model you would have chosen blue pajamas, but the sizes are designated to specific colors. Yellow is small. Grey is large. Navy blue is extra-large. Green is medium, what you requested so difficultly from Eunice. You're wearing a brown robe. You're not sure what size brown is.

"I am a writer," you say. You lie. You're actually a public relations assistant in a small resort community two hours north, but you've learned that having an interesting career often earns a patient better care. It's horrible to say, but there's fanfare everywhere, and more often than not people will err on the side of popularity or notoriety rather than take an unbiased stance. When it comes to the treatment you're unsure of receiving, you assume people will approach you and care for you better as a writer, an artist like Sam, than someone who writes press releases and promotes events for a living.

"Wow, a writer. That must be a fun job," Tasha says.

She's still smiling, and from the sliver of light coming in through the doorway you see a scar running six inches down the side of her neck. You wonder how she received this black weld of flesh. Was it intentional? Who or what cut her? Was she the type of person who was happy all the time because she found God, and in turn a new life or rebirth, or was she putting up a really good front. She persevered from something traumatic, is what you think, and her therapy is working with people who have yet to. You are uncomfortable with your chronic analysis of others when it is your analysis and rehabilitation you seek. More so, you hate the fact that Tasha's simple imperfection makes you appreciate her more.

"What type of things do you write about?"

You're not in the mood to answer any more questions, though you know the conversation could turn to her and this scar and you're intrigued. You could find out if the person who held a knife to her throat is in prison or if that person is free to roam the earth. If the latter; was she afraid? If it was something she did herself, did she see her life flash before her eyes? Did she die and come back from the dead like those stories you hear about on daytime television? But you are tired of talking. Tasha already asked dozens of questions after Eunice handed you off—some of the same questions Eunice asked:

Did you feel like hurting yourself?

Did you feel like hurting others?

Were you hearing voices?
Were you seeing things?
Did you do drugs?
How much do you drink on average?
Was there a history of mental illness in your family?
When was the last time you were hospitalized?
On a scale of one to ten, what was your pain level?

"The old guy already took care of my pain, evidently," you say.

Since your arrival you've revealed more about your personal life than you care to reveal again, but as told to you from all of those intending to help, you must. You must, to let the healing process begin. You must, to "build a dialogue"—something you remember from past hospitalizations. You must, so doctors can examine pertinent background information, whether it is physical abuse, injury, exposure or heredity. The more they know, the more you can grow, so to speak. You look up to Tasha and close your eyes. Your absence tells her you're done for the night and you say goodnight with the headache beating you into submission.

#

Before you fully wake, you take inventory of your surroundings. You keep your eyes closed and feel your lethargy flow from an injection site on your right arm. You swallow the metallic taste of medicine pooled in your mouth then lightly suck whatever drool escaped overnight. The side of your cheek and neck is damp from the evening's vegetative state. Testing your psychedelic paralysis, you clench and unclench your hands, running your open palms and fingertips over abrasive sheets worn thin. Toes curl beneath a thin wool blanket scratching an embrace. You open your eyes and see a wall papered in what looks like the inside guts of cardboard—beige and rippled. You see your breath blow white sheets in waves in front of your face, and the single bed beach on which you lay is a chilled draft of Lysol, bleach and urine, all succumbing to the same hot breath that flurries your sheets in surrender. You roll onto your side, an effort that takes a few minutes time, and you push up the sleeve of your green pajamas. You see a bruise and its pain deep in the tissue. You watch your heart beat in the violet circle and blink out of synch with your breath. You lie there, trying to recount every minute of every hour up to this moment, and you see your hand over your arm and notice how it has aged. These hands—ones that have labored and loved—look ten years older now, and you wonder if you do. You look around the room and see a wall locker, three additional beds (fully made), a stainless steel sink, a toilet and a radiator. There's a mirror above the sink. You want to swing your legs off the bed and walk to your reflection to witness years gone by, but you can't. Lying there, helpless, you wonder what medications could have given you this paralysis. You wonder if it is permanent. You wonder if maybe it is your will, or lack thereof. Finally, as blood replenishes a sleeping limb you rise slowly, every movement a hard exhale of exertion. Five paces, and a stranger looks into your eyes from inside the mirror, disappointed with the mask you choose to wear. How long have you had such a porous face? Have your eyebrows always been so thick and bushy? Nose hairs protrude, curled. You yawn and stare passed yourself back into the bed where you slept. You taste blood, open up and touch a tiny stream of red running between yellow incisors. How long have your gums bled? How long has blood pooled in your belly? You spit in the sink. You spit in the toilet. You kneel and watch the pink froth swirl slowly around your reflection cast from water the same shade as your teeth. A tear runs down your face and drops, rippling an image you have already grown to appreciate, as it's there you see your reality: the blood, the guts, the sense of who you truly are.

To your left is a solid oak door with stainless steel panels at the bottom and a wire mesh window running four inches wide, head-to-knee, near the knob. Where the door leads you don't know, but at this point the unknown feels better than the uncomfortable. You open it and peer into a white-tiled hallway: more of the same doors, stainless steel, wire mesh windows, same. Tiles run half a foot up the walls where light blue (not beige) cardboard-gut wallpaper is pasted. You step out and feel the décor—corduroy to the touch. You think of your jeans, you have two pairs brown and gray. You think of your clothes. You return to your room and open the wall locker. Empty. You look in the mirror once again expecting a new face only to find the same emptiness, only more tearful, more frightened. Your chin is wrinkled, clenched. Your lips quiver. Pitted eyes carry razorblades with every blink, and you want more than anything to keep them closed to avoid the pain of feeling, of seeing. You ponder myriad details that make up emptiness, and how.

Down the hall at a "T" intersection two offices straddle both sides. Across the hall and on the left a small office has a door open in halves, top and bottom. The sign on the top half reads "LPN." The bottom half has a table surface that rests on it as if it were a desk to stand at. Across the hall, on the right, is a larger office encased in glass, a fishbowl. On two sides the glass is drilled with holes to communicate with the residents of the ward. You call the drilled holes "strainers." You call them strainers because you have an overwhelming sense that nothing is secure or sacred here, which makes them more like sieves than anything. To your immediate left is a phone hanging on the wall. You pick up the receiver and see there are no numbers, no digits to dial. A sign above reads "Incoming

Resident Calls Only." Below that reads "Please Limit Calls to Five Minutes." You replace the receiver and walk across the hall towards the fishbowl.

"Excuse me," you say into the holes.

The two words are received with detachment. Three people who occupy the glass space look up and return to what they are doing.

"Excuse me."

A woman rolls her chair up to the window and mouths one word, a question. What? She offers you her profile waiting for an answer. You look at her jewelry; four rings on her left hand. She is married and loves Black Hills Gold. You make out patterns of colorful butterflies on her top, different sizes, different species, flying all different directions. In between two gold hoop earrings she readies her speech.

"What do you need?" she says.

On her right hand you see four more rings, more Black Hills Gold, not a single gem.

"Do you know where my clothes are?"[22] you ask. You have a good idea, but want to be sure. You want to know in the case you have to go home, and you feel as if you have to go home.

The woman runs her tongue over her teeth and sucks, swallows. Long fingernails, each decorated at the tip with a tiny butterfly, tap a drum roll on the counter in front of her echoing through the tiny holes and into a deafening silence.

---

[22] 2134 Resident Gisick awake for the first time since admission onto ward. Incognizant of surroundings. Janelle Sexton, RN, 06/06/09.

You look passed the woman as she looks passed you. You notice a wall clock behind her. 9:35.

"Honey, we have your clothes, don't cha worry 'bout them. You have to just wear what you have on for now, m'kay?"

You grasp your belly. Like you, it feels as if it's caving into itself.

"Did I miss breakfast?" you ask.

"Baby, you missed breakfast, lunch *and* dinner. You hungry?"

You feel the cold in the air you didn't before and tense.

"Where am I?" You know the answer but want to hear it from another's mouth. "Where is everyone?"

You suspect there should be others and hope there are. Where is the familiarity from the floor below?

"Sir? Sir?" you hear.

It's another woman, Jules' sister. She stands at your side, one hand holding a Dixie cup of water. In the other hand she holds four round pills; two red, one blue, one white.

"Sir, how about I sit down with you and talk to you a little while, tell you what's going on and how we're taking care of you?" she says. "How 'bout you sit with me in the common area right back here. I'll have Janelle get you a plate of something from the kitchen."

With a smile running across her face she nods to the butterfly woman tonguing her teeth again. You hear a hard slap of metal, what you expect are eight gold rings against a counter followed by two doors opening and closing, the fishbowl then the main door encased by steel grating. The smile from the new woman watches Janelle fly away angrily then returns to you. You'll call her Mabel.

Mabel leads you through the common area, a large vacuous room filled with items meant to distract residents from feeling they are anywhere other than where they belong. A wall locker of board games blocks out the sunlight set free from caged windows. Against the light it's a black hole, the only way out. Its contents stack high as if to suggest the ward's level of care taken for residents is superior, but box upon box repeating itself says differently. Checkers on checkers on Parcheesi on Parcheesi on checkers on chess and Battleship on Candy Land on Life on chess on Monopoly on checkers is a ward's way to admit redundancy is routine and the classic way to run things is business-as-usual. Expect the expected. You wonder if you are unique. You wonder if being unique is the most unoriginal thing to hope for in a place that shuns difference. The boxes stack high and topple every day, a game in and of itself. Pieces lie scattered on shelves with lost and missing cards. Gumdrop Mountain is in California, one resident will say. A yellow "Get Out of Jail Free" card will taunt others. You want to account for each game piece, there have to be 52 cards in a deck or you can't play. You feel as if you are one of these misplaced pieces, maybe a two of clubs. Other pieces will never be sought after or used: A pewter Monopoly thimble has long been swallowed, and all chessboards remain deserted and forgotten due to past bishops' visits to various human orifices. Mismatched vinyl couches— some rose-colored, some lime, some aqua—horseshoe around a 54-inch-screen television set in the corner at the far end of the room. More vinyl chairs the same colors, high backs most, line chipped and peeling walls (you will ask if the paint is lead-based) between bookshelves, also mismatched and old. One bookshelf looks like it came from your grandmother's bathroom in Fort Lauderdale. It holds a library of Reader's Digests, along with a few Hardy Boys and Nancy Drew mysteries, Louis L'Amour in paperback, magazines from the American Association of Retired Persons and the National Rifle Association—all laid out and sprawled open and torn, shoved onto shelves in no specific category, not unlike the multiple diagnoses that will run the halls during daylight hours. Every seat in the house, supported by worn, rusty springs ready to pierce through thin cushions, is aimed at the giant tube projecting the outside world 24 hours a day—only pixilated and accompanied by show tunes. Cartoon characters take turn being God here. Commercial jingles are Christ. Guests on talk shows are disciples sitting down in virtue like Leonardo Da Vinci's *Last Supper*, a print that hangs crooked beside the locker of games. Television personalities will be rejoiced and praised through this altar wired to a dish satellite aimed out over a gray landscape and grounds three miles from the nearest house, a half-hour drive from city limits. These made-up faces rule the outside world but have nothing to do with the people inside this cage. Even hope is a visitor here.

Mabel takes you to a corner of the room. She knows you need to feel you can trust. She knows you'll feel better with your back against the wall, though, figuratively, you feel like your back is against the wall too often. There you sit in a high-back chair beside a coffee table covered with pieces from

59

a jigsaw puzzle of a pond surrounded by a white gazebo and Adirondack chairs and weeping willow trees. You think of your youth when you used to hide under the protection of the neighbor's willow tree. You think of your adolescence when you kissed Susie Wilt under the same tree, not so much protection but privacy and secrecy. And those thoughts bring you up-to-date to remember that there were other women but there were more reasons women left. Among all your lovers the most devout has been failure, for failure has been consistent in your life. Failure never lets you down.

"Sir, let me tell you what's going on," Mabel says.

"I know what's going on. I'm in a hospital."

Your words are quick and slurred and lucidity is an inconceivable goal.

"All right, I suppose that seems pretty obvious. I won't play coy, do you know what type of hospital?"

Her hands are still cupped, beckoning you to acknowledge the medicinal rainbow in her palm.

"I know you've noticed the bars on the windows, and though I don't know if you tried to leave the unit, this is a locked ward. Specifically, you're on Ward 5-C, a unit for people who have been and still are considered unsafe to themselves and/or others," she says. "This doesn't mean anything other than that you're in a place to get the help you need."

You look around and hear her words repeat themselves, echo in your head. You see them float from her lips, bounding from Avon's Cherry Fire lip gloss to hover like movie credits in front of the big screen. They hang like a chimp's fingers around metal grating bolted to window frames, pulling thunderously to get out. They slide across the glass of the fishbowl and shoot down the ominous hall, morphed into a skeleton key, twisting to open and free themselves. You say nothing. Truth is freedom but it isn't for you, not now. You listen and watch her hands. When will she make her move to throw the medicine down your throat? Will the medicine make you smaller? Bigger? Who is the white rabbit you must follow? You grab your mouth with both hands. Did you just say those things? You don't know. You know very little at this point.

"I'm sure by the looks of things you're becoming nervous," she says. "You shouldn't be. If you are, I understand, but you shouldn't be. There's no need."

Mabel reaches her hands out, water and rainbows.

"You *should* take this medicine, though," she says. "It will make you feel a lot better. It will help you sleep..."

"How long have I slept? It's almost ten. I just got here, right? Right?"

Mabel retracts her arms, clasps her licorice fingers around the colored pills.

"Do you feel like hurting yourself? Do you feel like hurting others? Any hallucinations? Pain?"

She accepts you shaking your head in disbelief as an answer.

"Twenty hours," Mabel says. "You've slept twenty hours straight."

What documentation had begun, slowed to a mere pen

stroke of vital signs and the occasional notation[23], "asleep," every couple hours. Twenty hours, a thin medical file and starched sheets—changed twice from incontinence and defecation[24]—were your cocoon defining you. Twenty hours, and strange eyes trained not to judge watched over you tallying blood pressure, pulse, respirations, noting physical markings; eight tattoos covering arms, shoulders and back. The left forearm reads, "I am mine," so word passes to psychologists of possible narcissism. The right forearm and left bicep are foreign words, French and something Russian, Czech maybe. The right bicep reads "Jabberwhorl Cronstadt," and research says it is a nonsensical story written by Henry Miller, based on the poem *Jabberwhocky* by Lewis Carroll. Henry Miller is a misogynist and Lewis Carroll twisted, so must you be. A diagnosis you expect them to find from past visits to places like this only elsewhere rests in ink permanently emblazoned on your left shoulder, "Ecclesiastes 3:1-8," a passage suggesting life is a balance of duality. In your case, mania and depression is the balance you have not found, either teetering or tottering between highs and lows. But you know this, and you remain silent.

A plate of food arrives on a tray held by Janelle. Paste-white turkey and whipped potatoes covered in a beige liquid pool in

---

[23]   2200 Resident Gisick has remained in bed this tour. All rounds have discovered him asleep. Eunice Binoli, LPN, 06/05/09. Mr. Gisick in bed and asleep this tour. Richard Tyler, RN, 06/05/09.

[24]   2030 Mr. Gisick changed 2x this tour. 2x incontinence, 1x defecation. Mr. Gisick asleep during entire procedure. Janelle Sexton, RN, 06/06/09.

one rectangular compartment adjacent to a square dish of light green peas and another of apple sauce. The food is as lifeless as you and Janelle's look of complacency.

"Here's what you ordered," she says.

Her voice sounds better behind glass.

"I didn't order anything."

You talk directly to her butterfly print, a happier setting. She clears her throat (everyone clears their throat when they want to say something inappropriate).

"Thank you, but I don't want anything. I don't know..." You hesitate but she is there to pick up the pieces, not the pond and weeping willow of better times.

"You don't know what?" she asks. She leans over the tray of food. "You don't know I had to have the kitchen make this especially for you? You don't know I'm off my shift in ten minutes and I have a half hour of paperwork to do? What don't you know?"

Mabel calms Janelle down and, at the same time, urges you to eat. She asks Janelle to return to her station, finishup and go home. She says she knows it has been a trying day. She thanks her and apologizes on your behalf.

"You don't know what you're doing," Mabel tells Janelle, and takes the tray from Janelle, and sets it on the table between herself and you, hiding the freedom of flight.

"Why don't you eat, honey?" Mabel asks.

THIRTEEN

For years the only food you could to remember was Rice Crispy Treats. Your parents had plans to go out and celebrate their anniversary. It could have been their high school reunion or maybe a fireman's ball, you don't remember, but it being an anniversary gives more reason for you to be left alone. Thing is, you weren't left alone. You were in fifth grade, 10-years old, and your parents wanted to guarantee your safety. It wasn't "babysitting," you were too big for that term. Your mom made Rice Crispy Treats then called the Reynolds. Could Brian babysit? No, Mom, not babysit, rather watch, guarantee your safety? Yes, yes, he could. It was when the downstairs wasn't yet remodeled and the living room was upstairs, beside the kitchen. Your parents didn't go out until late evening and you already had supper. You remember eating the first of several Rice Crispy Treats.

When Brian arrived you said hello then ran into your room to hide the toys you still played with. Brian had a head for sports, so you made sure your baseball mitt and ball were out, Matchbox Cars out of sight. Dress to impress—no pajamas, shorts. You stood at the end of the hall and listened to your dad talk about football. How was practice going? Brian was the quarterback. He also played defense. "Iron Man Football" your dad called it. When you walked into the kitchen where your mother cut from the pan of Rice Crispy Treats and served Brian, you were sworn to good behavior. Be good, your folks begged. Don't burn the house down, they joked. You remembered the laughs, as if they were canned for sitcoms.

FOURTEEN

"I remember this place," you say, smiling under a memory.

Your eyes want to scan the room again, but you're afraid to take your attention off the food. What will Mabel do to it that Janelle hasn't already done?

"I'm not eating anything from here," you add.

Mabel looks at you blankly. After a quick glance to the plate of food, she returns her gaze and smiles. She says she doesn't blame you, then reaches in the deep pocket of her white lab coat where she releases the handful of meds and pulls out a can of dietary supplement, Ensure. Without a word she points to the closed flip-top lid and sealed mouth of the can and hands it over.

"I trust you can trust something like this?" she asks.

You nod, and she stands to leave you alone, making a final effort to distribute medicine. You shake your head and she returns to the fishbowl, humming a gospel song in full stride.

The evening is long and you can't sleep. You sit awake holding your can of Ensure, unsure of how your future will play out—not just tomorrow or the next day or the next week and so on, but the rest of this night. You sit staring at your silhouette cast in the common area's theater television and see you have no face. You are a profile of darkness and for some reason have more faith in that truth than any mirror or bowl of filthy toilet water. You think about how the tired man with luggage eyes told you the first day doesn't exist and how right he was. On the other hand, you think about this very moment and how much acclimating from the first day might have helped. Perhaps you'd return to your room at ease, rested. Perhaps you wouldn't think about what you expected from past experiences in hospitals such as these. Experiences strip-searched for safety, hosed down for cleanliness, deloused, examined head-to-toe for infection, all before a group of accomplices, all before being strapped to a bed in an isolation room, door propped open so an aide could watch over you—over pages of a magazine featuring more virtuous celebrities with relationship problems. Experiences with days of semi-consciousness, weeks of overmedication, and months of shame stemming from loneliness found being transferred from one abusive world back into another; the entire time remembering exit interviews as vividly as every intake—a day of saying goodbye to the familiar and once again stepping back into the unknown.

You open your canned meal and step up to the drilled holes. "Ma'am, I'll take those meds if you have 'em."[25]

---

[25] 2217 200 milligrams Sertaline Fumarate per Kelly Tesoro, Psych.D., 06/06/09.

FIFTEEN

The next few days, you adhere to a regimen of rest most new admissions are permitted. An unwritten rule on wards seems to allow new arrivals hours upon hours of sleep in hopes they become an active part of the floor's community in a couple days. At 5:15 a.m. you wake for vitals. Since arriving, there's been a retired serviceman working the graveyard shift who wakes everyone with a barking order trumpeted into every patient's room. You hear him begin his revelry each morning down the hall, slowly waking patients with solid raps on each door then a yelp that concusses with blunt force against the ears. You hear him on his way down to your door and before he can make a fist or lick his lips to holler you ask him to leave you alone loud enough that the rooms beside you wake. You will be there, don't dare touch the door. You resent the irony and know each morning's snap at the elder veteran results in documentation unbecoming of a patient, and it would probably be best if you allowed him to do his job, but you argue to yourself that you deserve the peace and quiet. You served in the military long enough to not be woken by boisterous folly and farce anymore.[26]

By 5:30 a.m. you're back in bed with numbers in your head. Your pulse is 58. Your blood pressure is 98 over 68. Your temperature is 98.8. On paper[27] you are healthy, and still you shake your head. Why couldn't there be a contraption to measure one's mind? What would it look for? Would it help people like Max to keep their jobs, pushing another machine monitoring the signs that remain vital to patients' lives?

---

26 0520 Resident Gisick raises voice to staff about obtaining vital signs. Argues that vital signs taken so early "don't make sense" and couldn't possibly be accurate especially when woken "rudely and abruptly." Sedative recommended for agitation. Patient refused. 06/09/09.

27 0526 Mr. Gisick's pulse is 58, BP 98/68 and temp. 99.8—running a slight fever, refusing suggested medication. Percy Livingston, LPN, 06/09/09.

#

The first few nights, you leaned a metal garbage can from your room against your door. It was your make-shift alarm. It woke you the fifth night on the ward, shaking staff from documenting and socializing to find you sedated and unable to defend yourself from another patient, a paranoid schizophrenic, who did nothing but stare at your paralyzed body and refer to you as his "brother."

"Brother, brother, brother."

He was short and balding and his breath smelled of sour milk. You could see nicotine stains on his fingertips, yellow and brown twigs, as he slid his hands on the bed towards your arms. The man's name is Clark—what two nurses yelled as he held your hand in his, repeating over and again, "Brother."

Lying in bed unable to move was life changing. You decided you didn't want to be that out of control. You didn't want to be hospitalized, but you didn't want medication to rule your life, either. Before falling to sleep that night you hoped you would remember to refuse meds until they found something suitable. As for the alarm, it wasn't good enough that the staff allowed it further. Instead, they documented on the incident and your increasing paranoia and removed the trashcan from your room.**28**

Regardless the can's removal, you create new ways of protecting self. At 6:30 a.m. you deny breakfast but pick up a can of dietary supplement. You pick up a second and third can at noon and 5 p.m., every time denying a tray of food and back-peddling to your room quickly and shutting the door. When the door is shut completel you take an empty Ensure can, the first one given to you by Mabel, and lean it against the door. You rinse each new can out in the sink and hide it hanging from the springs of your bed frame in case the first is confiscated for poor hygiene. You keep your eyes on the can and step backwards to your bed where you crawl up and curl into a ball, hugging your knees against your chest facing the door.**29** This single serving can of nutrition is your alarm

---

28 2213 After nighttime medication time, Resident Gisick went to room to ready himself for bed. In process, he leaned room's tin trashcan against door. Resident Clark entered room at approximately 2156 knocking can over and making loud enough noise to notify documenting staff member. Resident Clark was found in Resident Gisick's room calling Resident Gisick "brother" several times before he was escorted to the correct bedroom. Both Resident Clark and Resident Gisick fell asleep minutes later. It is this nurse's opinion Resident Gisick's facial similarities and physical likeness to Resident Clark's brother is an underlying contributor to his increasing agitation. Resident Gisick's trashcan was removed. Janelle Sexton, RN, 06/09/09

29 2309 Resident Gisick is found still awake lying in bed. When he noticed this nurse checking in on him he glared suspiciously. Janelle Sexton, RN, 06/09/09

against intruders. For the time being, it's all you can depend on—your nourishment, your safety. And in these moments of security, you permit yourself to fall into dreamland.

SEVENTEEN

There is something revealing and kind in Brian's care. Even though he is a man's man, six-foot-some-inches tall, lean and muscular, he doesn't mind that you want to build a fort of sofa cushions and prefer to watch music videos over the sports channel. He lets you help yourself to Rice Crispy Treats on the grounds that you listen to what he says and follow his direction. One of the instructions is to shower before bedtime.

"Of course," you say, unaware that he will insist that he help.

You stand naked behind a shower door watching the auspicious dark figure of your role model on the other side watching you. You swallow water from the faucet head to wash away the cottonmouth and listen to questions you have to strain to hear:

"Have you been in the boy's locker room yet?"

"Do you have to shower after gym in fifth grade?"

"Have you noticed if there are some boys that are more mature than others?"

"Do they have hair down there?"

Blowing air up from your mouth in through the force of water you wipe tears that have not yet formed, and you answer:

You know what a locker room is, but you won't start using one until next year or maybe after that. You tell Brian it depends on how much exercise the class gets during their lesson, and gym period is always the last period of the day so everyone would rather go home sweaty.

He tells you that's not good hygiene and uses the word "gross." You look at the bar of soap that's yours sitting in a dish damp but untouched and unlathered.

"Have you ever seen a man's penis?"

The water runs steady but the silence after his question is the quiet wake of an ebb and flow of commitment and hesitation. You want to shower forever, anything to avoid the silhouette behind the glass but you know with whatever you ask there are consequences, and you fear them. Despite wanting to not talk about the subject of physiology you tell him you've seen your father's but that was long ago, when you were a child.

"But you're not a kid anymore," he says. "You're practically a man yourself. What does yours look like?"

With your heart racing, you do everything within your power to not dignify your sex, the manhood he declares. Instead, you hug yourself under the hot water from where you see your towel removed from its rack and possessed by him. And from there you arrive in his arms to be dried off, caressed and sworn to secrecy. When your parents return home to find you sick, Brian is given a few dollars extra and you are scolded for eating too many sweets.

"That'll teach ya," your mother says.

"How are you going to be the athlete Brian is, eating all that junk?" your father says, shaking his head not once looking down to you in the fetal position on the couch beneath a thin crocheted afghan as vulnerable as you. "Well, you better apologize. This boy has bigger worries on his mind than a kid and a tummy ache. Go on, say 'sorry.'"

Brian refuses any apology and insists you stay put, relax. He has a game coming up and expects to see you cheering him on. He'll win a game for you, he says, as long as you do the same for him when you're older. And with a plate of Rice Crispy Treats wrapped in cellophane, Brian puts on his letterman jacket and closes the front door behind him, an unforeseen and invisible scar.

EIGHTEEN

It's been a week since your admission, and you have denied the past three series of medications.[30] You feel less sedated, but a fog blankets you and weighs down your eyes throughout the day. You make your way from your room to the commons area, not only for meals now, but to watch television and read. Before leaving, each time you close your door you place a broken straw from a broom high above, between the door and the door jamb. You suspect someone goes into your room each day, but know making any implication will sound symptomatic, so it's best to find proof—catch the culprit in the act. If the straw is on the ground when you return then suspicions are correct. If the straw is still in its spot then you will remain quiet. You are as unsure of your own sanity as are the people in the fishbowl, and if there's a chance a straw can tell you, you'll take it. For

---

30   0932 Resident Gisick has refused his medicine this morning. He has refused meds since yesterday morning, missing three medication periods. Kelly Tesoro, RN, 06/11/09.

another thing, it's less conspicuous than the trashcan or an empty Ensure can.[31]

You've learned from prior hospitalizations that there's a consistent ebb and flow between staff and residents on wards, and most times it's the pull of force from the powers that be that make a tide silky smooth or destructive. In Los Angeles, one nurse would take you outside on to the roof to play basketball. Plexiglas walls bordering the ledges were three inches thick and ten feet high with overhangs impossible to reach. The psychiatric ward was on the second floor there, in a hospital that towered nine. You once owned a pet mouse in college that ran a series of mazes and tunnels in a tiny plastic cage and you imagined you must have looked so similar to people working in offices above, an unkempt man in pajamas and robes hopping about chasing a ball bouncing from backboard to dust-covered walls as if searching desperately for a piece of cheese, a reward. On that same unit, another nurse used to deny men their cigarettes and revoke smoking privileges if they didn't clean their rooms. The task to clean was small enough to ask, but for some men that cigarette was the only reason to get out of bed each day. To stand outside pacing the Plexiglas border exhaling plumes skyward and tapping out butts in ashtrays displaced around the three-point arc was the one thing that brought them calm. They could have cared less about any form of cancer, their death was literally lurking over their shoulder;

---

[31] 0454 Veteran Gisick slept through the night, and did not barricade the door of his room. Eunice Bolin, LPN, 06/12/09.

they saw it as most people saw themselves in the mirror.

In Kansas there were marathon games of cribbage, but only with young staff that didn't know better than having fun with a patient was still work. There was a week of daily trips to the greenhouse where college students working internships as horticultural therapists believed you were on staff until seeing a wristband, at which point conversations changed as quickly as the Midwest turned winter, and you were suddenly left out, alone and shaken. And there was always someone each shift who read too deeply into your medical file trying to make assumptions about you, asking questions aside from the typical ones you received and making you feel worse than you already did—questions about divorce and children and run-ins with police. Even the tiniest inquiries reminded you that you were different and therefore categorized and watched over for your safety, not to mention the outside world.

What is it like to hear something that isn't there?

What *do* you hear?

What *do* you see?

Why have you named him Walter Dunn?

As most things in life, simplicity is experienced going with the grain, a direction you sought. You learn the ebb and flow can be a ballroom dance, but the key is deciding who is going to lead and what will be the accompaniment. You learn quickly that it isn't a full moon that brings out the lunacy in people but rather the people who believe that sort of thing and see a full moon as an excuse to provoke. You know more than ever that you are helpless when you want to voice your opinions, and they are deciphered through someone else's words and articulation in legal documents. You are your own advocate.

It's no different on 5-C. In the short time you've been here you've adopted a routine of inconsistencies[32] that are needed to not become totally complacent and dependent on the broken system promised to take care of you: the V.A. Depending on the staff, there can be times of normalcy just as there can be mayhem. It is best to go with the flow.

As with anything sedentary, there are factors to look out for to maintain one's health. Medication slows you, and even though you are off them for the time being, you exercise little. There is nothing for you to do except walk the halls and burn the calories that come packed in tin cans. The walk from your room at the end of the hall to the commons area is exactly 17 tiles. You know this because you have taken up counting to pass the time. You know there are 17 tiles to the commons area and 17 back, and if you count the walk across the hall there are eight more. This makes a lap exactly 50 tiles long: 17 down, eight across, 17 back, and eight across again. You turn at the fishbowl and count the tiles towards the locked entrance, past the shower room, then cross the hall and return the other way, past the conference room, past the locked door to the fishbowl, past the commons entrance and past the two behavioral rooms—one where Craig Crabtree, a patient of the highest

---

[32]   1758 Resident Gisick commented that residing on this ward was like a carnival. "It's like Las Vegas in here," he said. Richard Taylor, RN, 06/14/09

caliber, lies strapped to a bed and supervised by a male nurse with two diamond studded earrings. Cross the hall again and return, turn right at the community telephone and count to your door...144, 145, 146, 147. One hundred forty-seven tiles, each 12-inches by 12-inches, one-foot by one-foot. You do the math. Thirty-five, no, 36 laps you need to do for one mile. You feel your waistline, the pasty paleness of dough. You have lost weight but more so you have allowed toned muscle give way to fat.

You take the first step. By the third lap you already feel winded. You stare at the blocks passing beneath you and dream of flight. If you only had wings you'd never allow yourself to touch ground. You would float, ascending higher and higher. You'd find the cherub nurse and convince her that you are not a lost cause in need of a bed, then you would show her your strength and bed her. You shrug your shoulders, imagining what it might feel like to rise high and burst through the acoustic ceiling panels, the metal duct work, the coat of insulation and the concrete slab of the sixth floor, then onward and upward through the seventh, eighth, and so on. You watch the tiles swim below you and you slow your pace, thinking of all the people who would recognize your clothes and scream as if you were an escaped convict or a leaked contagion. On the sixth lap, the nurse watching over the ward's deviant and delinquent, Craig Crabtree, stops you. As he sets his magazine down, you ready yourself to answer questions. Since you've been walking, the charge nurse has already documented the behavior.[33]

"Were you ever a gymnast?"

The man is 5' 3" tall and has the voice of a thoroughbred jockey. He is a silver fox but balding enough that he should consider buzzing everything off, even the long wisps of gray that most certainly hang shoulder-length after a shower, hairs that are combed with the opposite arm back over the head and smoothed out with the hands. He looks as if he wears eyeliner and wears clothes straight out of the L.L. Bean catalog. He is pretty. He is your assigned nurse for the night shift—still, no doctor. It is his job to make contact with you and ask you questions about your mental status:

Do you feel like hurting yourself?

Do you feel like hurting others?

Do you hear voices?

Considering you know that you have a nurse assigned to you, you expect questions pertaining to things about your health, but there's more:

Did you do any gymnastics?

Do you work out?

You hear him loud and clear, but you're finding it hard that

---

[33] 1847 Resident Gisick continues on ward restriction status. Moved about the unit entire shift. Walked the halls at a rapid pace, reading while walking. He did watch TV with peers at brief intervals. No interaction or socialization with peers noted. Remains in the dayroom reading at this time. Will watch for further anxiousness and recommend anti-anxiety medication. Richard Taylor, RN, 06/14/09

these are legitimate questions during this one-on-one with him as the charge nurse.

"No," you say, though one year you did.

You're so entranced by what appears to be make-up around his eyes that you don't know if you answer him. You stare and hope he doesn't take your gaze as interest. You prefer to not place yourself in a situation which results in a discussion over your sexuality. You know this so strongly that you plan to bring it up if a doctor would ever show to speak to you, to speak to anyone, really. You continue walking.

"Oh, well it looks like you might have been a gymnast," he says. "You know, the way you're built."

His name is Taylor, Nurse Taylor. You walk past him, and he motions to an aide to watch over Crabtree as he accompanies you.

"Walking are we?" he asks.

"Yeah."

You wish he'd turn around, leave you alone, but there's no solace here. Despite being a respite for decaying minds to find clarity, you know there's a time when the banality of a ward does more harm than good. By this time you understand it's time to play the V.A. game—eat their food, take their meds, listen and talk and share. Though you have little faith in a system you have no choice but to embrace, you assume your empty vessel of a body can adhere to what is needed to get appropriate care and leave, try life again. You want Taylor to be on the same wavelength as you, to ask something that pertains to your health, something you want very much to not shake your head at. You want to know why it's approaching a week and you haven't seen a doctor yet.

"You're going to be joining us for karaoke tonight, aren't you?" he says. "You look like a singer."

His steps are in time with your own. The distance your shoulders are apart is enough to be considered intimate. You are a gymnast and now a singer. You understand the need to boost one's self-esteem when one is down, but there are ways of doing so without making it sound like a pick-up line.

And why, you ask, is karaoke night on the ward so much more important? You want to berate but haven't seen a doctor and fear any notes that might be taken by nursing staff will undoubtedly be mistaken as anger and violence. You've been right so far.

"Hey, now, karaoke is fun. It's all about having fun," he says.

His tongue is a little worm wiggling in and out of his mouth. He licks his lips before and after every sentence. He licks his lips in thought.

"Karaoke is a way for all the members to get together and be a community," he says.

He's a nurse who likes to whitewash the fact that people on the ward are mentally ill by calling them softer names, being politically correct. Since you've arrived to the unit Taylor's referred to men on the unit as "members" as if everyone belonged to the same club, Club Crazy.

"You'll see, it's a blast," he says.

You're only allowed to shave between 5 a.m. and 7 a.m. or 6 p.m. and 8 p.m. and since you enjoy showering with your shave you must decide to either do it early or late. Since you arrived you either slept in after medication time or were so preoccupied that you forgot to shower, and at this time your odor is offensive. You never recognized it until walking the perimeter of the hallways and somehow streamlining into your own draft gusting by. As you walk you lift open your shirt and see that lines of dirt mark your torso where folds of skin stack. You feel full and raised pores around your nose as black as the stubble on your chin and upper lip, an incomplete beard. The oil from your hair has formed acne in and around your hairline and you find yourself picking and pinching and squeezing, then looking for excrement on your fingernails. You walk another five laps thinking of how to break from Taylor, avoid pressure to be a "member."

"I have to shower. I can smell me and it's pretty bad," you say. "Can you unlock the shower room? I want to shave too."

"Sure," he says, again, with the tongue, two, three. "You're going to need me to supervise your shave though, okay?"**34**

You nod. No comments. No jokes. No help. No faith. The hard-working man you once were would call this "going through the motions."

"Okay," he says, cutting to the inside of the lap and heading to the nurses' station. "You sure you've never done any gymnastics?"

---

34 1903 Resident Gisick is done pacing. Refuses anti-anxiety med. Using shower to calm himself. This nurse will supervise shave. Richard Taylor, RN, 06/14/09.

You know most who have heard of stories about institutional-ization might relate the shower, a bath or any form of cleansing as a baptism—the washing away of sins, chipping away of guilt, devouring of evil. You know there are ideas of crazy men who believe they are John the Baptist or Jesus Christ and how these people with mental illness are those without any religion or faith and therefore undeserving of a laying on of hands. You accept indifference because at the very least it isn't hate. People think hate is the opposite of love, but no, indifference is. And with indifference follows apathy. Unfortunately, apathy is a steppingstone to bigotry and ignorance that leads to far greater crimes. You understand this is a large reason why psychiatry raises eyebrows, why counseling can be deemed shameful, why mental health units are typically locked, and why pharmaceutical companies throw psychotropic drugs at symptoms, not illnesses. It's simply one of those problems too big to handle right now. But you think of all the things you have heard on the unit from the many people from various walks of life imprisoned on this ward and how they need healed. How long will they have to wait? When they are visited upon, what will be their miracle? And there, behind an unlocked door in an eight-by-four room with a shower nozzle and a drain, you are once again vulnerable. You've stripped off your stigma, no longer a patient in green who resides on the fifth floor in the fourth bed of the loneliest corner room. You're as you came into this world, perfect and in the image of God. And you ask God why, as you scratch Brian Reynolds's name in the film of filth on your chest.

You've been told your stay on the fifth floor is strictly for evaluation purposes, but you know better. People—all veterans of different service organizations—come to the hospital and are admitted to the second floor first. After observation, these former soldiers, airmen, Marines are released back into society or relocated to other wards. The majority of these veterans are addicts. They use this time to rebound, sober up and reinstitute themselves as contributing players in the social world. Over ninety percent of these people will return, if not to this unit, to another in a different hospital in a different city. For some vets, hitchhiking from state to state and living homeless until either being dropped off or checking into the regional V.A. hospital is a pilgrimage. You yourself have been admitted to three hospitals, this being the fourth, depending on whether you are released or sent to another ward. Each place has been different and you've learned to look at each intake as an adventure and journey. Kansas, North Carolina, California and Arizona. Some people travel for sites advertised in tourism magazines; you have that and more.

Every afternoon, the common area is occupied by paper-shaded men dying from their own salvation.[35] What they believe will save them they allow to siphon their spirit. Bound in nightgowns and robes mid-afternoon watching daytime talk shows and courtroom drama on television, they burrow deeper away from society into a world ruled by Jerry Springer, Oprah, Judge Judy and medicinal therapies that either inhibit receptors or receive inhibitors, whatever the LPN is able to explain that day. They aren't men anymore. They are empty vessels with surnames used only when followed by the last four digits of their social security number meant to designate their specific prescriptions or dietary needs. Even their children have forgotten them, thus no reason for a visiting room with more than two seats. Nobody is ever expected because nobody ever comes.

One time your girlfriend came to visit you when you were hospitalized in Kansas. After four weeks, the doctors felt you needed to get off the unit for a while as long as someone took responsibility for you, so she signed you out like a library book and went to a movie. Halfway through the movie you told her you wanted fresh air, so you both left. All you did was watch television when you weren't reading. You wanted to go for a walk. The walk was short, as you were winded (one month

---

[35] 1534 Resident Gisick complains about the assortment of entertainment on the ward. "There aren't any current DVDs, only old VHS tapes. And your books are all romance novels. Even board games and puzzles are missing pieces. This nurse asked if he needed a sedative and patient denied. Richard Taylor, RN, 06/15/09

without exercise). Another thing you'd gone without was sex, and while sitting in her Camaro in the parking lot outside the hospital, you asked with little tact for her to oblige you:

"I need to have sex. I have to get this out of my system. Can we fuck?"

She stared blankly at you, at your hanging belly, your swollen neck, your jowls, your tearful blue eyes. She reached to your hand and held it, caressed it, then placed it to her mouth and kissed each knuckle. You thought this was a kind, yet roundabout way of saying no. You begged her to say the word instead of saying nothing at all until she placed your hand on her breast and ran it along her side, over her thighs and back up the inside of her legs to her own sex. Within moments you had her pants off, followed by yours, and within moments you were finished, unable to perform. You cursed the conditions—the car, the medicine. You rolled over and off her and saw her looking out the window at pillowy clouds you assumed distracted her from the catharsis you had forced upon her. She was angelic bedded under your apologies and there in front of you was willing but wasn't there. Her mind was elsewhere and her presence was with another. You tell her she doesn't have to visit to be kind. The hospital is taking good care of you, you say. You just need to adapt to the medication. It was the last time you saw her and knew it was for the best.

TWENTY-ONE

Of the men on the ward you share company with is Crabtree, resident bad boy, a different sort who's dying like the rest but proud of who he was and is. It's Crabtree, or "Crabs" as he insists on being called, who teaches you that seeing isn't always believing because some just don't have the right eyes. You see Crabs sitting alone on a sofa. You approach him and find him hanging his head over a *People Magazine* set beside him. His peppered beard is long and hanging over the front of his open robe. His right hand grasps the vinyl couch tightly, and his left hand is under his gown rubbing himself to full arousal. You see a beautiful young pop singer photographed in a bikini on the cover of the magazine then look up to the television and watch Oprah interview another beautiful young actress. You wonder who could be Crabs' fantasy, if anyone. You sit at a table behind him and wait for him to finish. You wonder how he's able to masturbate when you can't even get your penis erect.

"Holy Toledo," Crabs says, sinking into the couch, head back wheezing. "Shit, she was good. The tits, the ass, the hips I could sink my fingers into and bounce. Holy Toledo!"

You stand up and make sure he's addressing you. You've learned anyone could be talking to anyone in here. "Holy Toledo? Where the hell did you get that from? Is that an age thing?"

Crabs' Navy colored pajama bottoms are wet in the front. They appear faded around the dampness from other times semen has penetrated the same clothes. Chewed green beans hang from his beard and settle on his top, fallen leaves in a dying grove.

"Age?" he asks. "What you talking about age, there, bookie? Bookie, always got your nose in something trying to know, to do, to take over all us in here."

You've learned over a brief amount of time of Crabtree's schizophrenia, much worse than your own. You pray, and it is the only time you pray, that your life will not get that bad, that a solution will be found. Crab laughs maniacally when he gets on a roll, but he's wise enough to keep his voice low as to not be heard and risk sedation. Like you, Crab hates missing out on anything and would rather battle insomnia than nap.

"Hey, preacher man, *I'm* the entrepreneur, you see," Crab says. "We were baby killers. We didn't stay as one because of bamboo cages or wooden splinters under our nails, but you... You have to pass on the word and you can't find it in these goddamn books. You need King James Version, not fucking Gideon or Jack Mormon..."

You glance at the fishbowl and don't see any movement that would suggest they hear Crabs' growing agitation. He watches you turn from his attentiveness and throws his fists onto his knees in anger.

"I'll buy up all the tobacco in Virginia and I'll sell watermelons in New York, then I'll get into the housing market and start selling some houses. *You* need to get yourself one of my fucking homes, but you know what? I'm not going to fucking *sell* you one, and you can have one over my dead body, book man."

With that, the fishbowl empties out and floods around a man who only needs to talk out his demons. Fear, yes, there is fear in facing down anyone who isn't in the same consciousness, but the only way to see it and understand and survive is to believe it exists.

But nothing other than order exists on Ward 5-C, so Crabtree is removed, strapped to a gurney of apathy. Muscle holds him down and a small-gauge needle enters his shoulder, liquid sleep. He fights enough to stir the waters on the ward, making all staff as nervous as during full moon's rise. **36**

---

36 1932 Resident Gisick is kept under careful watch since companion, Resident Crabtree, was sent to isolation for behavioral problems. Richard Taylor, RN, 06/15/09

TWENTY-TWO

The morning comes quick. At 5:15 a.m. the room is still midnight and a silhouette of someone you don't know stands at the doorway. Before you can sit up and wipe the sleep from your eyes, the figure is gone. You close your eyes to be woken as soon as your lashes meet.

"Sir, it's time to get up."

It's Sam. Her hair is thick and white and hangs over her shoulder onto your cheek she is so close. She wears bifocals with multi-colored frames and peers into your face without making eye contact. She stares into your pores so it seems.

"I need you to get up," she says. "The doctor would like to meet with you before breakfast."

As quickly as she appears, she walks off towards the door, her hair falling behind her into a thick brush dignifying her as not only an artist but a tool to work with. You wish you could see what she sees from this place.

You are hesitant to get out of bed. You know the first picture the doctor is going to get of you is one of destitution. You don't have time to shower but you grab a simple toothbrush and squirt the fluoride-rich toothpaste on the bristles. You pace your room running your mind through scenario after scenario. If you are released, how will you cope at work?[37] How will you explain your absence to your supervisor? How will you look anyone in the eye? At the windowsill, you watch the sunrise over peaks Tasha named and you've long since forgotten. You watch a city come to life, stretching busily down long avenues that you know remain parallel, intersect at a horizon. You see the all-night diner beside the 24-hour gentlemen's lounge extinguish their night's welcome glow and the parking lot below fill with people armed with backpacks and morning drinks. You count the length of feet of shadows in guesstimates based off the length of your pinky. The convenience store's sign has a shadow approximately 30 feet long. The auto mechanic's shop, 15 feet, maybe. The homeless man pushing the shopping cart packed full of cans and blankets has a relatively small shadow, only six feet, or half a pinky. At this time, you feel everything is as it is supposed to be. The sun creeping over hill and mountain tops, revealing every fragment of your being through beams kissing your face, an aged frailty, a snowflake like no other and melting.

"Can you see me?" you call through whispers. "Can you see me looking down to you?"

Your forehead leaning against the icy surface of the glass,

---

[37]   0604 Resident Gisick asks about job opportunities when he leaves the ward, says he is "anxious to get back to making a buck, again." Will advise Veterans Trasition Services. Samantha McCannis, RN, 06/16/09

tinted against the eastern light, you plea to whoever will listen. And with the fingers from your free hand, you again measure a world from which you are disconnected, tracing the path of cars, stopping buses, blocking out office buildings and lifting bodies to the sky.

In the commons area every seat is taken: couches, chairs, arms of chairs, tabletops and windowsills. You settle for standing, leaning against the big screen Sony television in the corner. You glance at the only wall clock in the room see time stand, like you, still. Steady as sloth, time travels five, ten, fifteen minutes past and nobody has come to let the patients know what is going on.

"Hey," you yell to the fishbowl. "Why are we out here? What am I doing standing here?"

A man in casual clothes, an aide, glares, turns his back and walks to the bowl entrance. You watch him mouth words to his school and swim to you.

"Listen all of you, the doctor is doing her rounds in the ward next door. When she is done she will come visit every last one of you. Why you are here is to meet her to get help, because she's busy... Well, I can't help that... She can't help that... You're the ones that are sick so maybe you can."

You stare until you see the second hand tick backwards.

TWENTY-THREE

When your parents came home that time when Brian watched over you, your mother blamed your illness on eating too many sweets. Well, it wasn't sweets that made you sick to your stomach, and it wasn't a football injury that destroyed Brian's life. That was only the beginning.

In the homecoming football game against a neighboring town, Brian threw a pass as he was being tackled and smacked the ring finger of his throwing hand on the helmet of one of the defenders' helmets. He played the rest of the game, and the team chose to run the ball more. The last time he ever threw the ball was a toss in obvious pain that not only ended in an interception but was rumored to cost him a scholarship to a junior college—somewhere he didn't care to attend anyway. After the game, it was apparent either his finger and or hand was broken. The hand that had once touched me was blue, and the finger was bent at a 45-degree angle overlapping his middle finger when he tried to outstretch his hand. He held it gingerly against his chest, in front of block number 12, his number.

An hour later, he was back home, as was I with my parents.

It was there I learned of karma.

"Well, Brian, if you would have finished doing the yard work we asked you to do you wouldn't have been punished," his dad laughed.

"That's right, Dad. Laugh it up, basketball season is right around the corner," Brian said. "Your football god has just pissed off my basketball god."

Brian looked at you out of the corner of his eyes, and his Adam's apple bobbed down and up with a swallow only you recognized.

"I bet they just splint the finger, maybe cast it, but it will be more than ready to go in a couple weeks," your father chimed in.

By this time, Brian was an older son to him. He was everything you weren't, and already approaching adulthood where commonalities were far greater. You remember looking to your mother, but she was in deep conversation with Brian's mother, which left you to your lonesome and to disappear into your imagination where Brian was injured worse or where he was forced to admit his wrongdoings before you and God.

If given the choice, your parents would never know; out of fear, they would think you were even weaker. It was one reason they never knew when you were hospitalized. The stay at the Reynolds home was short-lived that evening because Brian's parents escorted him to the hospital emergency room to have X-rays taken. For a month his fingers were encased in plaster, and for the rest of that year I never attended any high school event. My mother worried about my bleak social life, and my father hoped I wasn't going to become a couch potato. I never told them why it was I sacrificed a year, just as I never asked Brian why he sacrificed me one night. The last time I saw Brian was the day he graduated. There standing with his diploma in hand, robe unzipped and tassel flopping from side to side of his cap, he extended his hand to me and smiled. It was at that point I saw the fear in his eyes, a mirror of how I must have looked less than a year ago.

It was my folks who told me not so long ago that Brian—after graduating from college, finding a successful job, marrying a beautiful woman, and fathering two wonderful boys—was struck by God with an inoperable brain tumor. All he had was time, and a limited amount at that.

TWENTY-FOUR

Seated beside you is a patient, member, veteran whose name is always called before yours. Alphabetically backward, perhaps. "Mr. Warren" to the staff, "Rosie" to you, he introduced himself three days after his admission. During that time you gave him time to adapt to the new environment and accept the temporary conditions of his life. You let him shed the burden he carried, the guilt of happenstance on the outside, and watched him evolve from a depressive introvert with wisps of brown and gray hair stuck to damp tearful cheeks into somebody who enjoyed small talk and walking the floor for exercise. When he seemed comfortable, you made eye contact and smiled. You asked him if he wanted to watch a movie and he said yes on grounds that the movie was funny. You told him you wouldn't have it any other way. "Mr. Warren" received five phone calls during that first movie, and when you mentioned how popular he was he only returned his concentration back to the movie as if you didn't exist. That same night, after a dinner of lukewarm chicken breast and beets, you built the courage to ask Rosie why he was on the unit.

"What's the punishment?" you joked.**38**

What you learned was no laughing matter, but rather something mournful. This was Rosie's fifth suicide attempt.

"I can't get it right," he smirked, two buck teeth setting on the outside portion of his bottom lip.

He tells you he's crying out, it's just that the people listening don't understand.

"You know me, Mom," he says on the phone that night. "If I'm not thinking about suicide, I'm doing it."

He has convinced you that thinking about suicide is a way to stay alive, because as long as the thoughts are there, the person won't do it. When the thoughts disappear, that's when the shit hits the fan—Rosie's words.

---

38   0937 Resident Gisick inappropriately jests at Resident Warren's multiple suicide attempts. Samantha McCannis, RN, 06/16/09

TWENTY-FIVE

The doctor has every patient on the unit present in the community room. Every seat is taken and, like a briefing to soldiers you've attended so many times before, you are one of two dozen strange faces dressed alike looking to a leader expecting some form of guidance. This leader—the psychiatrist you've been waiting for—steps lightly to the front of each man, looking down at them. She introduces herself with a Polish name (one you can't repeat without reading in bold letters floating on an imaginary marquee before you), but you later learn she hails from Argentina. She's short and her accent is lazy, as are her auburn eyes and the violet eye shadow dashed over each lid. Her gaze is an orchid, but the soft petals hide a wasp's nest of fury and spite.

Behind her are a handful of younger faces holding folders and taking notes. Rosie whispers to you that these are resident doctors in the psychiatry program. They are from a nearby university. He adds that this psychiatrist's sessions are done in an open forum not only to expedite—your word—the process but give the students a broader view of psychoses up close.

"I feel like I'm in a fucking zoo," Rosie says.[39]

"What kind of animal would you be?" you ask, hoping to add some levity to what appears to be an anxious encounter for Rosie.

The doctor—holding a to-go coffee from a convenience store in one hand, and the other hand hidden in the pocket of her white lab coat—looks to the audience of patients and announces a new name. "Mr. Krause... Gerhardt."

Gerhardt? You didn't know his first name was Gerhardt. A few nights before, an elderly man by the name of Krause asked if you would read the Holy Bible to him. He said he didn't have any education and hearing the verses from "the good book" eased his anxiety. At the age of 88, he was hospitalized for aggressive tendencies at the nursing home where he and his wife of 69 years resided. Aggressive tendencies that you understood were rumors and nothing more than subjective documentation from staff. Once again, your truth was different from their truth. You tell him you would read the only verses you could relate to, Ecclesiastes 3:1-8, the permanent reminder of lessons learned tattooed on your back. Afterwards, you told him, you planned on taking a nap. You were exhausted from doses of medicine you were prescribed but have not taken for months.

"Oh, thank you so very much," Krause said.

Stooping over where you sat, he handed you the Holy Bible, and you thumbed through its pages. Long ago, you studied the

---

[39]   0946 Resident Gisick continually interrupting Morning Meeting. Samantha McCannis, RN, 06/16/09.

bible and at one time thought it would be something you would do forever. During university, you thought about becoming a minister. You would have been a priest had you been raised Catholic.

"I'm not a good reader," he added. "It takes me a long time to get through anything at all."

Krause stood 6' 4" crouched, a monster of a man with hands that palmed the book he chose to live his life by.

"What are you doing in here, Krause?" you asked. "You seem calm, a gentle giant sort of man."

Krause sat down in a chair behind you and you turned to face him. His face was a prickly pear of gray stubble and his thick eyeglasses hung from the bridge of his nose. His hair was parted on the right side of his head, cultivated rows of white.

"I don't know, exactly," Krause said. "I was mad because they wanted to take my Dottie away. She ain't doing so good, and they wanted to put her in a different place. I don't like being without my Dottie."

You learned that Krause and his wife met in North Dakota. Krause's father bought a cow from Dottie's father, and during that exchange, a hint of love between two teens blossomed. Before you read, you listened. You listened to a love story that outlasted blizzards and recessions, one that was as strong as the gold links that bound their fingers and united them in marriage nearly seven decades earlier.

"You'll see her soon," you said. "I don't imagine you being held captive much longer."

You turned your attention to the passage you were to read,

but Krause was up and walking out of the community room.

You were looking through the titles of movies the ward had available: all VHS tapes pre-1998. Krause returned, and you were excited that at the very least you'd have something to draw your attention away from the tools of boredom that had been bestowed upon you for your own suffering.

"I haven't crapped in three days," Krause said. "My stomach is as hard as a rock."

You held out the Bible as if to invite him to partake in a study but he was preoccupied on the condition of his bowel movements.

"I'm all stuffed up. Can't go."

You walked to the nurses' station and tapped on the glass.

"Excuse me, could I get a nurse to look at something?" you asked. "Rather, could I get someone to look at nothing?"

The staff didn't understand the humor and it troubled you they hadn't documented a positive mood change. Then again, you weren't so positive yourself on what each notation said. Up until this point, everything had felt controlled, purposeful under someone else's guidance. Now that you wanted control of your own, you felt tumultuous repercussions. At the glass window they even asked that you not mark up the windows to the station.

"We don't appreciate having greasy smudges on the glass, so if you could please refrain."

"I will refrain, if you could please exorcise the shit from my friend's intestinal tract," you said, a third time for poor humor.

As your memory replays the comic antics of Krause, the

doctor finishes and looks back to her group, a mixed sort of young adults you knew had their own private dramas intermingling among each another.

"All right, who's next?" she asks.

A boyishly handsome-looking man in a lab coat steps from behind a serious girl who had yet to look up from anything she wrote. With a file in his hands, he steps to the side of the doctor and declares his charge. "I have a Mr. Warren, Roosevelt."

"Roosevelt Warren?" the presiding psychiatrist repeats.

Rosie raises his hand, hesitantly.

"Mr. Warren, how are you today?"

The doctor sips from her coffee and approaches slowly while the domesticated menagerie of students remain at the community room's entrance, their quickest escape from the curiosities they are so enchanted by.

Rosie clears his throat as everyone does when they are readying to defend themselves. From his periphery, he watches men he may not have served with in the military, but still considers comrades here. Faces of lambs most, with the occasional lion—it's times like these shame grows and words dissipate. Fear is herded, fear feeds fear.

"Mr. Warren, how are you feeling today?"

This question, asked infinitely during institutionalizations, is only an antecedent to generic therapies. The doctor, in a tenured malaise, knows she will ask questions to no avail and what was once an investigation intent on healing the inflicted becomes a textbook treatment written decades ago and still practiced to this day.

You look to Rosie and see the fire in his eyes is all but extinguished. His head lowers to his lap and his hands fold into one another, a prayer.

The handsome student opens the folder and, as Rosie did, clears his throat. As if at a podium delivering a commencement speech, the student surmises Rosie's medical life through annotations from days prior.

"It looks as if Mr. Warren is admitted to Ward 5-C for...," the doctor begins, turning an Argentine accent over and over her tongue. "...let's see...suicidal ideations...found in his apartment..."

You nudge Rosie in hopes of making him relax, maybe smile.

"Hey, me too," you whisper. "I was found in my apartment too. But mine was a shitty studio, I win."

"Mr. Warren, this is your...fourth time?"

"Fifth! Fifth time!" Rosie speaks, and turns to high-five you. **40**

His voice reverbs against the glass of the nurses' station far behind the students, startling not only a few of them but the patients beside you.

"Calm down, Mr. Warren. All we're here to do today is discuss how you felt that constituted staying in the hospital, and since then, how you have felt since your admission. This should be really easy for you, right now."

---

40 0958 Resident Gisick celebrates the attempted suicide of Roosevelt Warren with said patient. Samantha McCannis, RN, 06/16/09

The doctor smiles and takes a sip of coffee. A half moon of lipstick eclipses the lid of the cup. Her lips roll into one another and smack and a smile returns, then silence. The student returns to his dictation but is stopped.

"No, let Mr. Warren express himself. We sometimes just need to give time and space."

Rosie says nothing. The doctor steps toward him and, as if in a showdown, lifts the cup of coffee to her lips once again before setting it down beside an unfinished game of dominoes.

Krause is up and shuffling to his room, a dose of Metamucil has kept him regular, inadvertently making him go more than he cares to. The student steps back behind the girl still engrossed in her studies. And you bounce a gaze back and forth between two entities that had yet to understand one another—not only a doctor-patient relationship but service-serviceman, country-countryman. In hindsight, you ask yourself whether you would raise your hand to serve. If you knew your fate, what would you do?

You remove yourself from the two and look among the other patients on the ward: people you know at this time, people you know you'll see again if things in your life don't improve, people you'd rather forget.

In seconds, you gather what professionals could never in years: Krause and Rosie will live for a long time. Krause will return home and even after his wife's complete submission to Alzheimer's Disease, he will insist on caring for her until her death. He will pass on, only days after she is received in Heaven. Rosie will return to the hospital one more time, until a son of his own makes an attempt on his life and is hospitalized. At that time, he will gain strength he never thought he had and become the man he never knew he could be.

Other men will die weeks after their release. (Alcoholics Anonymous Meetings and Narcotics Anonymous Meetings where addicts have choices to attend do nothing for the drug abusers who enter these doors.) Free room and board topped with tongue-in-cheek sincerity does nothing for the former service members that the hospital truly wants to rehabilitate. A guised whimper stuttered through detox wins the hearts of many, but it's the addicts' hearts that are torn after further abuses. Eventually, it's a body that gives—either theirs or someone else who tires of the addiction, often dealers who play to the veterans' needs, some addicts before exiting the military.

And there's you: sober but sick from medicine that promises to heal you, to rid voices, visions and lay straight rough waves of manic-depression. But medicine can't be a cure-all.

"Hey, Doc, why don't you lay off!" you yell, your voice cracking under pressure. "Why do you think he's not talking? You have all of us out here to hear his shit, and all of these people behind you... It's a lot to admit to. That's a pretty big assembly, don't you think?"

The doctor spins on her heels of black patent leather.

"And you are?" she says.

"Someone who would rather not share my story with everyone in here," you say. "We all have our own stuff."

You slide your hands into the pockets of your brown robe and clap them together in rhythm with a nervous tapping of your feet.

"Mr...?" She asks, lagging the word, waiting for your answer.

"Gisick, 2938."

"Well, Mr. Gisick, if you would appreciate private counseling..."

"This is supposed to be counseling?"

You know this question has toppled any authority the doctor felt obliged to pride herself on. This ward is hers, and you have desecrated sacred grounds. She turns to a nurse and asks that she remove you from the meeting and, under supervision, stand you outside her office until her rounds with her students are done.

You watch Krause re-enter the community room from the restroom and step in front of the doctor blocking any hint of her out from sight, dwarfed by one of your own. You look to Rosie and wink and the only thing you can say comes from a deodorant commercial.

"Never let 'em see ya sweat, Rosie, my man."[41]

---

[41] 1035 Resident Gisick openly mocks the ward's Morning Meeting, at the same time urging other residents to question administrative and therapeutic staff members' standard operating procedures. Samantha McCannis, RN, 06/16/09.

TWENTY-SIX

You stand outside a room that the rotating staff of physician's assistants, psychologists and psychiatrists use as an office. Inside—you've seen it before—there is nothing but blank white walls, black filing cabinets and gray desks assembled from a single page of directions and an Allen wrench. Everything is simple, a contrast against every case that sits before the people who call this room theirs. No picture of the wife and kids, no honeymoon photos with the husband, no posters of favorite professional teams, let alone a personalized coffee mug. On the far wall, there is a poster of a soldier geared up for Operation Iraqi Freedom, and underneath the poster a sign that says, "It takes courage to admit you need help." Opposite this, above your head, you read about the indicators of stress, titled with two words printed bold in orange and all capitals, "WARNING SIGNS."

The doctor finishes her rounds and enters the office, followed by a man you have never seen before. After a few minutes you are called in and sit down in the only chair available. You pull your brown robe up above your buttocks and lower yourself onto a firm cushion.

"You are here, why?" the doctor asks. She sits at her desk, a heavy steel government-issued desk with a thin Formica top. The distance between you and her consists of little more than an 18-month desk calendar and supply organizer filled with pens, highlighters and paperclips. She looks over the fresh coat of red wine nail polish at the tips of her fingers then strums them against the arms of her chair. "Can you tell me?"

This is a process you've gone over time and again. If you could relive the first mention of how and why you ended up here, you'd see yourself in front of Max who first took your vitals and smelled of morning. Then there was Jules and, of course, Annie before them both. You remember Eunice and Tasha and you remember every nurse during every shift who asks the same questions, forcing you to relive each humiliating moment like a poorly run AA Meeting. You know who you are, and you don't want reminding. Fix the problem, you beg—but first, the problem.

"Mr. Gisick, you really need to work with us," the man says, never introducing himself but standing close enough you can read the name on his badge that's attached to a lanyard around his neck—Mark Boswick, LCSW. His white shirt and khaki slacks are pressed neatly, and his shoes (burgundy wingtips buffed to a shine of cabernet) are worn thin on the bottom, suggesting his hard work ethic. "We're giving you the opportunity you wanted, so let's have it."

"Mr. Boswick is right. We're stepping outside normal protocol to take time and hear your concerns," the doctor says.

"In essence, you're getting special treatment, something the other men on the ward have not received."

"That's for sure." **42**

It feels like an eternity to hear her sentences—long casts into a deep lake waiting for a strike—but you strike first. She turns her head to look at the man who is standing in the corner jotting notes into a beige leather-bound folder.

The man looks at her over his glasses, his forehead a wrinkled staircase to spiked strawberry blonde hair. His eyes fix on you, he clears his throat and swallows hard.

"Mr. Gisick, as we understand it, you came to us after contemplating suicide," he says. "Now, we're trying to help, and to help we need to know more about you and the extraneous circumstances surrounding your life. It's as simple as that. The only thing we have to go off of for the moment is what nurses and staff have told us, but what's going to do you justice are your own words."

Your own words. For the longest time you've thought you've been speaking your mind, but you have not. What you have been doing is speaking the mind of someone unclear, unfocused. To be understood clearly one must first speak to be understood clearly, which means having a mind to begin with. Being addressed so carefully and told to use your own words shakes you sullenly. This is a new feeling, you believe. It is permission to be courageous and decide one's own fate. **43**

---

42 1103 Resident Gisick presents himself as an agitated, yet reserved patient, concerned with conditions on the ward. Mildly sarcastic and disrespectful towards his ~~superiors~~ treating staff. Mark Boswick, LCSW, 06/16/09.

43 ~~1114 Resident Gisick is asked repeatedly, "What can we do to better the system?" to no avail. Patient remains silent after several attempts at communication. Mark Boswick, LCSW, 06/16/09~~

TWENTY-SEVEN

You cross your left leg, foot resting on your right knee. You switch, lifting your right leg to rest on your left knee. You switch one last time before placing the rubber soles of your slippers firmly to the ground, pushing your back against the vinyl chair and sliding up from a slouched position. All is quiet until you are settled, an auditorium sitting patiently listening to the string and brass section of an orchestra warm up. You've waited so long and now it's time to speak your peace. You've waited so long, what is there to say?

"It's fairly obvious why some people are here, hospitalized here, some even living here," you say, addressing the doctor. "Whether they don't know their ass from their elbow, or just need a place to crash and come down off a two-week drug binge, this is the only hope for more people than I care to imagine."

An uneasiness falls over the room.

"Well, it seems…" begins the doctor.

"No, ma'am, I'm talking. You asked me to talk, so I'm talking. Don't interrupt when I might not get the courage to talk again. This isn't easy."[44]

The room's tension is matched only by thumbs clicking tops of pens, retracting ink-damp tips, and pencils falling on yellow legal pads, a momentary reprieve from documentation.

"Ironically, to me, this entire experience is like Dante's *Divine Comedy*, and the ever-so-popular phrase, 'All hope abandon ye who enter here.'"

"And how is that? Can you share with us?" The doctor's pristine hands and beautifully manicured fingertips fold over each other, swaddling delicate and carefully chosen words.

"Yes, I can. I'd love to share," you say, wiping a tear welling up in your eye. "Everything is a joke, and chronic record-keeping of the joke. I'm supposed to come here and get better, not share my exploits to virgin residents in lab coats—exploits, by the way, that categorize me as a certain type of character who's defined in one of your desk manuals or handbooks. I'm supposed to, as everyone in here is supposed to, come here and get better, but how can anyone get better in an atmosphere like this?"

"What do you mean by 'atmosphere'?" Boswick says.

"I'm still talking... It's been assumed that I need help, and I go along with the diagnosis and prognosis, and whatever other

---

[44] 1129 Resident Gisick has called for a private meeting with Dr. Glomski and this LCSW. Patient states he would rather not share his personal feelings with strangers who are not trained in the field of counseling or psychiatry, and believes it's not healthy for other patients to hear the complaints or issues of others. Patient's demeanor is aggressive and defensive. Mark Boswick, LCSW, 06/16/09

'-osis.' But where is the cure? When do I escape the terror, and begin to embrace life? Can *you* tell *me*? And before you answer, let me add that your questions are condescending: 'And what do you mean by that?' 'What do you mean *atmosphere*?' Get over yourselves. Get over yourselves and that piece of paper that deems you an authority over me." **45**

The man's throat clears until the doctor breaks the grumbling with a moment of sincerity. "I think you have a point, sir. We don't know what it's like to be you. We're fortunate to leave work every night and have a home to go to. We aren't here at all hours, and we only see our patients during scheduled times. As far as us being condescending, I don't feel that's true as much as I think it's an exhaustion we also feel. We'd love to sit down with every one of our patients, but time doesn't allow it, especially when we each have hundreds of cases. This isn't counting the new cases that come in each week."

You listen to the doctor, noticing she isn't wearing a wedding ring, wondering if she'd take you if the man wasn't in the room. You wonder if that's the only reason he's in the room, and you begin to feel angry that you're not trusted.

"I'm not questioning your competency," you say, "and I'm not questioning why each of you chose psychiatry or social services as a profession. I'll assume you wanted to make a difference in the lives of people in need. That said, let's look

---

45　1137 Resident Gisick is having difficulty defining his current diagnosis, not to mention his present status on the ward. He shows signs and symptoms of paranoia, living in an alternate world. Mark Boswick, LCSW, 06/16/09

at my life, your patient-in-need. Aside from prescribing me a drug that will alleviate some of the depressive symptoms I experience, what else will you do?"

"Why, we'll—"

"No," I say, "let me answer that. I'm still talking and would appreciate the chance to express myself."

You stand up from your seated position, an abrupt move that frightens the man. You backstep toward the door so they take you as a threat.

"You'll make sure I'm adjusting," you continue, "to the medication, that is. But that's half the problem. The medication you prescribe treats the symptoms, but it should be curing the disease."

The doctor leans further back in her chair, slides her hands into the pockets of her lab coat. You wonder if she's hiding a stun gun, maybe something to alert security to detain you.

"I'm sorry you have to hear this," she says, "but psychiatry is an old science that has a lot to do yet, to catch up with the illnesses it is designed to treat. Considering there isn't a cure for the common cold and there isn't a cure for balding, it shouldn't be a surprise that there isn't a cure for a multitude of mental illnesses. That's easy for someone to say who isn't struggling with the disease, but it's the truth."

"I appreciate the truth."

"Then you should appreciate the fact that we want all the ailments under control until we find a cure for the actual illness. I suppose the theory is that we should be doing something, right?"

You lean back against the steel door, feel the cold ripples of latex paint layered on decades ago. Your eyes scan the interior of the room again, they translate the frigid loneliness.

"Whose office is this?" you ask.

"Everyone who works on the ward, except the physician's assistant and aides use this room, so in a sense it's communal," the doctor says. "Why do you ask?"

"It's just that everything is so generic, as if nobody has any plans on staying here too long—as if everyone is a transient mental health worker, paying their dues before they move on to a private practice."

"It may *seem* that way," the doctor says, "but we're very intent on treating our patients. We consider ourselves the best treating the best. And trust me when I say, I wish there could be another way of treating you, but standard operating procedures call for a pharmaceutical regimen, first and foremost."

"Don't get me wrong," you say. "I'm glad pills can dam up my waterworks, and I'm ecstatic I won't be sniffing around to get laid by any stranger every night. But in the long run, without these milligrams, I'm as good as fucked—quite the irony. I'm not just limp-dicked, fat and tired, I'm fucked. Who's going to hire me? Who's going to want to associate with me?"

"If people can't accept you for who you are, then why have them as friends?" the doctor asks.

"Because I have so few, and the company would be nice."

Boswick writes furiously in his binder, but the cant and angle of his hand suggest it's out of frustration and could be nothing to permanently note in your medical records. The secrecy raises your level of nervousness.

"See, you have me talking right now, but I know damn well it's over when I'm out of here," you say. "There's no therapy. There's no counseling. And there are things I need to get off my chest, I'm sure of it. I just don't know what those things are just yet."

"I'm very proud that you're able to talk openly about your feelings—"

"Spare me the public service announcement. I know as well as you, it's inconceivable that there's enough manpower to do anything but diagnose, document and distribute drugs. It's like you said about priority—drugs first."

"I might have alluded to that, but those weren't my words."

"I'm a number like the thousands of other patients that walk this hospital. Literally, I'm a number—you know me from my social security number. Worse yet, you'll never get to know the real me, I'll soon to be doped to the gills, so as not to talk back again."

The man's cell phone rings. He scrambles to turn off the blaring ring tone (MC Hammer's "Too Legit"), and spills over a stack of files beside him. He apologizes as he fumbles with the phone in search of a menu to silent it.

"I'm so sorry... I... sorry," he says, dropping the phone in his pocket and returning his attention to documenting.

"Hell, I might be a pretty decent guy," I continue, "aside from the—what is it?—'episodes,' as you call them? Aside from those, maybe I'm a good man."

"Sir, you have to know this isn't your fault," the man says.

"Should I know this is something that *has* fault though? I mean, my diagnosis is something that gives me fault... Is that what you're saying?"

"No, not at all..."

"Why can't the world accept me for who I am?"

"I don't think it was *the world* that sent you here," the doctor says. "You came of your own accord. And that's one of the wisest things about someone in your case. You've recognized that the illness contributing to certain conditions isn't healthy. You coming here is a huge step, and we're here to help you along the path. I'm sure you've heard what I'm about to tell you a hundred or more times, but it's true. When you have a headache, what do you do?"

"I drink water."

"Drink water is one way to get rid of the headache, but what else? Do you ever take aspirin or Tylenol?"

"Yeah."

"And if you've banged up your knees playing softball?"

"I play baseball, and I'd ice them."

"I think you see the point. That point being—if there's a malady, there's also an answer. If there's a problem, there's a solution."

"I understand what you're saying."

"Do you? Because if you did, I have a feeling that you'd take the medicine you're prescribed, understanding that it will alleviate the problems you're having. Again, this is no different than taking ibuprofen for muscle aches or nitroglycerin for heart patients... "

"But ibuprofen doesn't make you fat, and aspirin doesn't kill your libido."[46]

"Are those things you can manage?" asks the doctor. "How important are they versus maintaining a healthy lifestyle? How important are they versus staying alive?"

"You're treating the symptoms, not the illness," you repeat. "And now that I've complained about my weight and lack of mojo, you'll want to treat those. Gotta keep the troops happy, right? Do you have any other answer aside from meds? I'm not pointing fingers, but after I leave here—which I would like to do today—will you see that I receive the proper counseling? Will I be able to address the issues that brought me here in the first place? Probably not. Why? Because, there's no room for it. There's barely room on the wards, let alone in the files that define us. And there's no room for our kind anywhere."

"You haven't answered my question," the doctor says. "Anyhow... What do you mean by that—'your kind'"?

"Look around. Are you blind, or have you been here so long you're numb to the entire experience in a similar way your patients are?"

"I still—"

"Yeah," you say, "you're still and I was. I'm not sure what it says in my folder you've got there, but I was a pretty extraordinary man once. Before college, I could throw one helluva curveball.

---

46 1138 Resident Gisick complains of weight gain and lack of libido. Look into possible medications with the pharmacologist for prevention and assistance, i.e. diet programs, Mark Boswick, LCSW, 06/16/09.

The bottom would drop right out of it. In college, I had my first son. I took a full class load and worked 40 hours a week, while raising my son. In the military, I learned Arabic. And after language school I became a combat medic then flight medic.**47** My first trip to the hospital came after I told a friend I wanted to jump into the rotor blades of a UH-60. His answer: 'Who doesn't? It was at that point I didn't want saving, I didn't think it mattered, or that I had taken the ugliness of my life as something more than it was—turning anxiety into something terrifying and life-altering."

"I'm sure you led an amazing life."

"I 'led' an amazing life, eh? Past tense," you say. "Anyhow, did you know my first stint in the hospital was five weeks?"

"We've all read over your file, Mr.—"

"Five weeks of feeling like an insecure adolescent, not knowing where I'd fit in—if anywhere—doped up, drugged up, allowing strangers to fix me with medications, never reassuring me that I was good enough. To this day, I need to read affirmations on my fucking bathroom mirror to know that I'm a decent enough individual to do some good in this world."

"And you are—"

"But instead of counseling, you'll give me a cocktail of pills to swallow three times a day, right?"

"Every patient is different."

"I have a name."

---

47 1141 Resident Gisick is exhibiting signs of narcissism and slight aggression, symptoms of psychosis. Mark Boswick, LCSW, 06/16/09

"Of course, but—"

"Never mind. Did you know that I've held a dozen jobs since leaving the Army?"

"No—"

"I've mopped up after geriatrics in a nursing home. I've been a landscaper. I've been a telemarketer. I've worked in customer service. I've worked as a stage hand. I've been a bouncer. I was an activist for Save the Children. I substitute-taught a few times before becoming a full-time teacher at a private boarding school where I taught English as a Second Language and coached soccer, basketball and baseball."

"It's apparent you're quite intelligent—"

"You think this lack of stability is based on intelligence?"

"Well, history has proven that some great minds have had some forms of mental illness, some very much like what you've experienced, and they've contributed great things to society."

"Let me stop you right there," you say. "Every time it's come up that I have this...this illness, people pull that shit on me. I hear about Oscar Wilde, Van Gogh, Abraham Lincoln, and a dozen others. But let me remind you that you need only peek into the community room during dinner and watch the handfuls of men devouring processed food and watching Judge Judy to know it's a far cry from this genius happening to more than one out of a thousand inflicted. And now, let's say the odds are greater. Let's say seventy-five percent of the men drooling over their peas and carrots are geniuses. You're going to put them on medication, if you haven't already. The great minds of previous centuries didn't have the meds, so how can you make this a fair comparison. It stands to reason that we'd be better off not taking meds and instead running for public office or inventing shit that comes off the top of our heads. Any thoughts on that?"

"It's a good argument. But let's think of those people who suffered and probably didn't need to. You're right when you say society either sees mental illness as a creative bonus or disadvantage. It seems there isn't a perceived middle ground."

"Let me tell you why you're letting me go home tomorrow—"

"The chance of you going home tomorrow is slim," says the doctor. "There's a lot of paperwork to file, and staff to consult over your case, and—"

"Are listening to yourself? Paperwork is the reason you won't let me go home to be around the people that love me."

"From the sounds of things, there haven't been too many people who have loved you."

"Did you really just say that?"

"I did and I apologize. That was uncalled for."

"The fact of the matter is that it's true," you say, "but it doesn't mean being locked up with other miserable people is any way to treat someone. Using the same practice of thought— prescribing medicine to rid people of traits that are normally frowned upon—it stands to reason that groups living in a mental institution should be euthanized, depending on the severity of their illness."

"All right. Can we start over? I don't think we got off on the right foot."

"No sweat. But understand, I am going home."

"Why is it you want to go home?"

"I'll answer your question with some of my own. First, where's the most dangerous place for an alcoholic?"

"I'd venture to say, a bar."

"Second, where is the most likely place a person gets sick, home or a hospital?"

"It depends—"

"I'll answer for you: The hospital, the place where people go when they are sick."

"Where are you going with this?"

"My point is, I'm not getting healthy being surrounded by people asking me to read the Holy Bible to them, telling me the size of their bowel movements, talking about attempting suicide three thousand times. This is not a place for respite. This is not a place for recovery. This is a place mired in memory, reminding everyone in here that we are subservient and crazy, if not just plain stupid."

"Well, you certainly did articulate that well."

The volley of debate carried on so fluidly that you never realized you had stepped aside to let the man out of the office and take the second call to his cell phone. The conversation grew intense enough that you didn't notice the marks your fingernails left in both of your forearms.

"Are you sure you're fine?" the doctor asks, seeing you trying to smooth the indentations out of your skin.

"I'd be better if you allowed me to leave," you say. "No offense against you and your staff, but I want to surround myself with people that know me and love me for who I am."

Locks of red hair fall off the doctor's shoulder as she turns her head and reaches for a pen and pad of paper.

"Come on, doc... I just finished bitching about the meds. No more, please."

"I'm not writing a prescription. I'm asking you to give me phone numbers of three people you will regularly see when you leave. I'm going to call them and ask them to be my eyes and ears. It's something I've never done before, but may be something I recommend to hospitals in the future. I'll consider it a deterrent, a reminder of how awful it is to come in here when things suck. It'll be up to you to make that choice. If I see you in here again, well, I know your plan didn't work and we'll go back to the basics."

Without your cell phone, it's difficult to remember three phone numbers of people you consistently associate with and aren't afraid to share your treatment with. In time, though, you have three phone numbers written down and hand the pad and pen back to the doctor.

"Okay, there's a couple things left to discuss," the doctor says.

"Shoot."

"First, you're leaving against my advisement, which means you'll have to sign a waiver relieving the staff and hospital of anything that happens to you once you walk out our doors."

"Consider it done."

"Second, though we don't have psychologists or psychiatrists in your area designated to talk to you, there are some inexpensive therapies I'd like you to look into. One is a group therapy—"

"Fuck that."

"—and one is a one-on-one. I'm giving you information on both. I'm giving you phone numbers, contact names and addresses, hoping you will select the best one for you."

"Can't I just do rocks, paper, scissors?"

"With who? Yourself?"

"Ha ha! Good one, doc!"

You sit down, relieved to unload the burden of honesty, guilty that your relief has now become another's weight. The doctor reads over the phone numbers as if checking their legitimacy, making sure none were prefixed with 555. In the brief silence, you feel it's necessary to share something, yet you're worried the doctor will be insulted at an insinuation which sounds so much like advice.

"Hey, doc?"

"Yes."

"I know you can't understand what it's like to be a person with a mental illness, just as I can't understand what it's like to be responsible for their care. At the same time, I'm not naïve enough to think nobody, no matter who they are, has ever experienced some horrible stuff. I've dated women who've been molested when they were just school children. I've had friends who had they fathers kick the shit out of them on a daily basis. I'd never ask, but I imagine you probably have your own demons in your closet, just like some of the staff on this floor. That said, I have a request, something that would take more than signing a waiver or giving you a phone number."

"How do you say it... Shoot."

"Well, consider taking your interns, whether they're from psychiatry, psychology, social services or nursing, and have them experience what we, as patients experience."

"How do you mean?"

"During their schooling, have them endure a week locked on a ward. Make them wear cheap pajamas and sleep on shitty beds in rooms that smell like Pine Sol-over-piss. Make them eat three meals a day served out of a steel crate on wheels by shady men in hairnets. Make them attend AA meetings, three a day, and sing karaoke for entertainment. Give them grade school word-finds to pass the day, and VHS movies produced from the 1950s to 1980s. Limit the shower-room hours, because that's where violence and fucking happen, sometimes at the same time. Dose them with sleeping pills and antihistamines three times a day, but don't let them sleep the day away. Watch over them and write about everything you see them do, say, feel, despite never truly knowing. Get in their heads, and get it wrong. Make them live a week in our slippers and offer them the opportunity to learn empathy. Do all this, and make us human."

The doctor pushes herself from the desk and stands up. She approaches you, kneeling down and placing her hands on yours, folded together on your knees.

"I know this isn't easy, but trust me when I say we know what's best."

"Trust. *Trust?* Really?" you say. "I've loaned out my body for how many years, only to trust the V.A. and their rules."

"And it's those rules that will keep you safe. It's these laws that will keep you alive."

You lean close inches away from her face, threatening to kiss her, threatening to strike her with your forehead.

"In heaven, there is no law."

TWENTY-EIGHT

What seemed a lifetime after Brian changed your fate, his too changed. The day of your exit interview from the hospital, a phone call comes in. Only two people know you are here. The call comes from your best friend, the man who brought you in. Someone in the family has passed on, he says. You panic. Who is it, you ask. You hear the name, "Brian" over the receiver. The only Brian you know is a friend of the family's, not your friend. What did your friend tell your family? You ask.

"Don't worry, I didn't let on you were in the hospital. They think you're out camping where there's no reception, no nothing," your friend says. "I'm supposed to go get you and ask you to head home for the funeral."

"How did he die?"

"They said it was cancer, he had a brain tumor."

"I know."

"If you knew, then why ask?"

"I mean, did he suffer?"

There is supposed to be an absence of any description with the word "numb." If it were to be described as it properly suggests, there wouldn't be any adjectives to precede any limited nouns associated. There wouldn't be any adverbs following the few verbs of little action. But ironically, numb is probably one of the greatest feelings there is. It is great because it renders both stimulating and dulling sensations. It's when an appendage has no feeling yet small tingling pricks vibrate all over. It's a word on the tip of the tongue. It's describing love. It's describing indifference. Religions might refer to numb as the alpha and omega, but you believe it is solely a vacuum of emotion infinitesimal in pain. It's where you are and all the forks in the road you took to get here, and detours you wished wouldn't have been and what you could have done to prevent from taking them. It's hindsight. It's foresight. It's being forced to deal with what you're dealt.

You ask again. "Did he suffer?"

"Come on, man, that's—"

"I asked a question: Did he suffer?"

"I don't know. I'm not going to ask, but I'm sure you can imagine. I'm sure you know it couldn't have been easy."

You say nothing. In your silence you debate what wish to make: to be patient and learn to forgive, or hope Brian's agony equalized what horror you've since felt.

TWENTY-NINE

It's the day before you return home and, judging by the oily prints on your window, it's easy to tell your interest in the outside world is growing. Every morning, a man from housekeeping comes in to your room to sweep and mop and wipe clean nightstands and windowsills. With the same rag he uses to dust, he runs the width of each window, reaching as high as he can tip-toe, removing opaque splotches; forehead, finger, and nose. The first few mornings you hear him enter, you hide your face, embarrassed that anyone other than a doctor or nurse see you. You peek from beneath covers but only observe the man's backside. You can't make out his looks—whether he is older, honest, loved. You can tell he is a black man and he wears his uniform with pride: chocolate brown work slacks and tan shirt pressed with starch. You can't tell what faith, if any, he observes, but he stands at the window farthest from your bed, overlooking the desert city most every day. It is his religion. From the fifth floor there is much to see and you don't blame him for taking in the scenery. You imagine it is inspiring for those open to such things.

This man leaves the room every time he cleans but only for a minute, always returning with a hot cup of coffee that he places on the windowsill fogging up the glass. And there, as the sun rises and you rest swaddled in a thin sheet and blanket, he consumes his cup of Joe and the morning. Every so often he removes the rag from his back pocket to wipe smudges he tends to miss during his cleaning. You watch all hints of your existence disappear as smoothly as he sips at his coffee and you wonder why forgetting couldn't be so simple. Why couldn't this man enter your life and look over it as he does the desert out in front of him, erasing the reality that keeps you tucked away and afraid to even say hello? You'd tell him thank you for cleaning the room. More so, you'd tell him thank you for the company, and for the hope. You'd ask him to pull up a chair, you don't mind, there are more views from other windows. Every day another exits and another enters. Wards such as these are a revolving door, infinite illness seeking endless empathy. You don't have answers, especially being here empty-handed with no resources, no assistance. What you can presume is that there is hope for everyone. Whether it's the shower that cleanses or the individual who stands by impartially doing the right thing and clearing up the tiny smudges in life, it depends on where a person stands and how they look at things. And here you are, writing these words on scratch paper taking in a million-dollar view, trying to find the beauty.

No, you don't mind, because these are small episodes of your life, and you're learning to accept them. And as is anything numb, you surmise there is the mincing of two meanings within your life, in turn, conflicting quality. But at least the hallucinations are under control, and the rollercoaster ride of emotion is not at risk of derailing, according to conversations with your doctors.[48] Of course, a lackluster empathy vies against the want of the company the voices provided. And so begins that conversation, almost a hallucination—that voice nobody hears but you, the one-sided debate with self, the one reason for leaving the hospital, almost.

---

48 1107 Veteran met with the treatment team this a.m., Dr. Hasselling, R. Lichtenberger, PharmD., Ms. Stephenson LCSW, and this writer. Veteran states that he is still having racing, unfocused thoughts. Medications discussed with veteran and he did not rule out the possibility of taking a stronger mood stabilizer medication or other medications as an outpatient. He requested written information on all pharmaceuticals prescribed, which a unit nurse will provide for him. Resident states that he is eating better. He will now eat food from his dining tray as opposed to when veteran first came to hospital and would only eat packaged foods/drinks. Veteran remains very suspicious of others, states that his wife (unaware if, in fact, he is married) told him that he sent his resume to the CIA and is afraid they will enlist him. Advised not to enlist in CIA, and work on progressing health; mental and physical. R, Licthenberger, PharmD, 06/18/09.

THIRTY

You can count the beats of your heart behind closed eyes. You stand and whisper a nursery rhyme in time with the pressure, until a voice behind you asks you to clear the way.

"Make a hole, man!" the voice hollers. It's raspy, thick as tar and rugged. "You just gonna stand there making tunnel rats like myself wheel around ya?!"

You open your eyes and watch a wheelchair speed around you. The driver wears black fingerless leather gloves and a bandanna the color of the American flag. A long gray braided ponytail hangs low, blocking out letters of an embroidered patch sewn to the back of the chair. Old English block letters read "SOBER RIDERS," a motorcycle group of 12-steppers. Two smaller patches—a POW and American flag—are sewn below. The driver stops at an ashtray in the breezeway and trails his index finger through sand and ash the color of the man's hair. You watch him as he picks out one, two, three, four butts and drops them into a white-and-blue cigarette pack wrapped in cellophane.

You pace the outdoor breezeway careful to avoid any people

who might make eye contact. One's eyes say it all. They are the mirrors to the soul and, since broken, you feel cursed years beyond the benches and archway that contain you. Beyond the broken melody stuck running over and over is the idea that all eyes are one you. You are a statistic. You are the most recent. You, the newest member of a heavenly craziness.

Two young women lead an elderly man away from his seat on a bench. One holds the arm of the man, guiding him and an oxygen tank wheeled in front so slow that you have to stare to guarantee any movement. The other, empty-handed, walks behind carrying a weight few can imagine.

You sit. Your clothes are tighter than when you first arrived. A body you don't recognize has amassed over your muscular frame. You had to rip yourself from pajamas to pour yourself into belongings you barely recognize. The t-shirt isn't yours; it's a navy blue pre-shrunk cotton t-shirt. XL. It smells of dust and cedar and antiseptic. You unbutton the top button of your jeans. Rub the impression in the dough of your stomach. Rub it from red to pink to a pale flesh tone you swear the ward's fluorescent lights burned upon your skin. Let go of your stomach and feel it descend into the canyon teeth of your zipper.

At your feet is a paper bag filled with orange translucent bottles wrapped in white labels. Inside each one are voices commanding rules and regulations required to safeguard you against something you've learned to hate: you. Tiny typed text stands out as big as a billboard, each one a chemical combination or compound echoing emptiness jarred against capsule, pill, and tablet. Each bottle is an elliptical portal to a world you

146

have only tasted but will soon depend upon. Each taste-turned -dependence is a reminder of words spoken through you only hours before returning you your clothes and unlocking a door for you to leave. The words are an echoing diatribe, a one-sided argument that snaps in synapses and chimes the cerebellum.

"You are about to re-enter the real world but this time with the tools to make you a more functional part of society: We've established who you are but in order to make you more successful—and we can't truly expect that—you need to heed the following pieces of advice, consider them for the rest of your life, your standard operating procedures. We know it works from this point forward."

You reach into the bag and pull out a series of pamphlets and brochures. You run your fingers over photographed characters of every gender and ethnicity staged in patriotic poses. You try desperately to wipe off fingerprints smudged on the glossy film of sharp-edged rack cards. You try frantically to rid greasy violations smeared on the inanimate, but the more you wipe the hazier the image.

"Every person is different; people with your diagnosis need medication; these are the medications that work best for people like you. Take 150 milligrams of Sertaline Hydrochloride**49** each

---

49   0947 WARNING: Antidepressant medications are used to treat a variety of conditions, including depression and other mental/mood disorders. These medications can help prevent suicidal thoughts/ attempts and provide other important benefits. However, studies have shown that a small number of people (especially people younger than 25) who take antidepressants for any condition may experience

day, these are the blue pills the size of Skittles, but sometimes orange and small like Tic Tacs. Take a half tablet of Quetiapine Fumarate 300 milligrams,**50** one half in the morning, the second half in the evening; there's a pill cutter in the bag we're giving you. Take 2000 milligrams of Depakote each day, but separate them in two doses—morning and evening—1000 milligrams each dose or 500 in the morning and 1500 before bedtime because you would not have had anything to eat and it is a medicine that doesn't sit well on an empty stomach; you have the option of using Depakote, either white or orange tablets, or the generic brand which is cheaper but in soft capsule

---

worsening depression, other mental/mood symptoms, or suicidal thoughts/attempts. Therefore, it is very important to talk with the doctor about the risks and benefits of antidepressant medication (especially for people younger than 25), even if treatment is not for a mental/mood condition. Tell the doctor immediately if you notice worsening depression/other psychiatric conditions, unusual behavior changes (including possible suicidal thoughts/attempts), or other mental/mood changes (including new/worsening anxiety, panic attacks, trouble sleeping, irritability, hostile/angry feelings, impulsive actions, severe restlessness, very rapid speech). Be especially watchful for these symptoms when a new antidepressant is started or when the dose is changed. R. Lichtenberger, PharmD., 06/19/09.

50   0950 WARNING: There may be a slightly increased risk of serious, possibly fatal side effects (e.g., stroke, heart failure) when this medication is used in elderly patients with dementia. This medication is not approved for the treatment of dementia-related behavior problems. Discuss the risks and benefits of this medication, as well as other effective and possibly safer treatments for dementia-related behavior problems, with the doctor. R. Lichtenberger, PharmD., 06/19/09.

form called Divalproex SA;[51] both types of medicines contain Valproic Acid which requires food or milk be taken."

You throw the brochures in the trash bin located beneath a concrete ashtray and reach for any other propaganda hospital staff might have issued you. There's a magnet the size of a wallet with hotline numbers asking you not to hesitate if you feel suicidal. The image on the magnet is of an eagle perched on a dead branch of a nondescript tree. You wonder about where eagles nest and what types of trees must be there but are resigned to feeling flightless, wings clipped, caged. Even a pulse seems too much to ask.

"Don't think of this as a coping mechanism; block out

---

[51]   0955 WARNING: This medication has rarely caused serious (sometimes fatal) liver problems. Children less than 2 years old are more likely to develop severe liver problems, especially if they have metabolic problems, severe seizures with mental retardation, brain disease (organic) or if they take more than one drug for seizures. If divalproex sodium is being used in patients with these conditions, then it should not be taken with additional anti-seizure medications. Liver function tests should be performed before and during treatment. Early signs of serious liver problems include vomiting, unusual tiredness, swelling of the face or loss of seizure control in patients with seizure disorder. Tell your doctor immediately if you develop any of these symptoms. This medication has rarely caused severe (sometimes fatal) disease of the pancreas (pancreatitis). This problem may occur at any time during therapy and may worsen quickly. Tell your doctor immediately if you experience stomach/abdominal pain, nausea, vomiting, and loss of appetite while taking this medication. This medication can cause birth defects. Discuss the risks and benefits of this medication with your doctor, especially if it is prescribed for a condition other than seizure disorder(e.g. migraine headache). R. Lichtenberger, PharmD., 06/19/09.

any stigma that might alleviate the stressors in your life; you are Bi-Polar and Manic Depressive, not crazy.**52** Monitor your behavior; keep a journal and note your mood, whether or not you feel overly sad and depressed or elated like when you do with women or spending exhorbent amounts of money. Avoid relationships; don't mistake lust for love; don't find comfort in sex; expect a decrease in your libido. Find a support network."

You spend the next fifteen minutes watching people enter and exit the front of the hospital. You scan each wrist looking for a watch so that you may ask the time. The last person you spoke to was the friend who admitted you. You called him after you were told you were ready to leave. He will be picking you up soon. Or was that just your imagination? Were you ready to leave?

"Don't forget medication; forgetting medication risks relapse, and you don't want to return here. There are plenty of

---

52 As of 06/19/09 the patient is deemed stable for discharge from the inpatient unit. He has been evaluated though short of stabilized on the medications listed above, insists on dismissal. It is the recommendation of the treatment team that he be placed on convalescent leave until medical discharge can be obtained. Transportation has been arranged through the military unit to have him picked up from the hospital and transported back to post where he will be evaluated by the post's mental health team. His medications should be continued on an outpatient basis, and his stress level should be kept to a minimum. Should the patient decide that he wishes to pursue some individual therapy to develop more coping skills as well as work through adjustment of having a chronic mental illness he would be good candidate for individual dynamic psychotherapy. R. Lichtenberger, PharmD., 06/19/09.

medications to try in the future but stick to the ones we have given you and let us know how you feel."

It's nearly noon. You haven't eaten. You glance once again at a bottle and its prescription and directions, realizing you have to medicate yourself now. Time is of the essence, or so you believe. Or so you were told. You look in your pockets— nothing. All belongings are in the bag. You refuse to reopen the bag again. You are intimidated by the sunset hues and the stars they contain. They are supernovas, bright in their degeneration.

"The medications you are on can damage your kidneys, pancreas, and liver."

You think about life outside of the hospital. People won't know what happened on the inside except from what they see on the outside. "Get in where you fit in," a drill sergeant once said. You look at the doors to the hospital. Are they an entrance or an exit?

"You will fit in better. Establish a routine and follow it religiously. Begin each day not by getting up at the same time, rather by going to bed early the night before; begin each evening not by preparing for sleep, rather by winding down after the day then rise regularly each morning; use nighttime to recuperate from the day and understand excessive alcohol inhibits the ability to rest, as does caffeine and sexual promiscuity; use daytime to savor the energy saved from a good night's sleep; use the night not as a venue for promiscuous activities; try meditation; yoga; acupuncture."

You walk to the trash bin beneath the concrete ashtray and

reach in for the brochures and pamphlets you threw away. The pictures and words are your identity. Without them you feel spineless. Without them you are a broken compass over a torn map, lost at sea, capsized.

"Here is a list of phone numbers of agencies—some charitable—that will help you get back on your feet. If you need transportation to your residence, we can arrange that. If you need to make an appointment there is a shuttle service free of charge. If you need dietary advice we recommend calling this number. Again, the medications you are on can be damaging to your kidneys, pancreas, and liver, so watch the alcohol intake; we recommend abstaining from alcohol. Stay away from drugs."

A white truck pulls up to the curb and honks. Your friend jumps out and greets you with a hug that bends you backwards. Marshmallow skin is compressed and slowly inflated upon release. An exchange of words, one-sided perhaps, and your belongings are taken up in his hand. A door is opened and you find yourself crawling into the passenger seat. Once still, he closes the door and walks around the truck. From the side view mirror you watch him peer inside the paper bag at the bottled infrastructure that is you.

"We recommend abstaining from sex. The medications you are on will cause a decrease in your libido. Do you have anyone to go home to?"

Your driver, a friend you recognize but looks at you like a stranger, asks if you'd like to go out to eat. His mouth moves and you see "...decent non-hospital food..." escape his lips. Your head moves. Yes? No? You only wait to see where it is you go. Ten minutes of quiet and you sit in the truck parked beside a gas pump. You hear "filling it up," "something to drink" and "it's going to be all right." Everything is quantitative anymore.

"Let routine be your religion; allow steps be your god. Make lists and obey them as you would the Ten Commandments, even if there are only six things to do throughout your day. Don't put too much on your plate; you have a lot to deal with. Break the monotony of your routine with time spent doing the things you love. You don't want to come back to this facility but we are here with open arms if you need us. Here is a toll-free number if you have any other questions."

You find yourself holding a Dr. Pepper in your hand and are torn between gratitude and irritability. Yet another doctor is helping you with your meds, and now the once sheer enjoyment of soda will be left with the memory of a metallic aftertaste. Tic-Tac and swallow. Pen cap and swallow. Three thumbs of chalk and swallow. Deny the difference—today.

"Any questions?"

Accept the numbing sensation. Toes and knees tingle. Fingertips curled in, retracted talons. Nodding off, you watch the desert roll alongside your peripherals. Saguaro cacti have surrendered long ago, as have sagebrush pinned beneath steel guardrails guiding you northward. What you once called the sky in which candy-apple balloons rose and fell over amber hilltops ablaze with olive sage is now a canvas of floating Rorschach clouds casting shadows over cookie-cutter neighborhoods filled with the Dick-and-Jane and Jack-and-Jill and that nameless point-four that teeters on the discussion of conception. Tire tread is curled in its fetal position on autumn asphalt, torn from its revolution evolution, a black withered rind of a watermelon discarded since July. Ravens pick at the intestines of the winding road's sacrifice, and winds from trucks 20 miles too fast kick pelts into the sky to fly off with infested flies.

In the bedrock of landscapes as differentiated as the people among them exists remains of life whose decadence and destruction will forever be contemplated. And in those skeletal remains or fossilized fragments, there is hope that you too will be pondered and pontificated. What was your life about? What led you where? Did it even matter? To know but one day in the world you once lived and mattered, because you cannot forget to remember...

Yet it is worthy to ask one to remember to forget.

"Son, this is your life."

And you set your eyes on the skyline cut jagged by the frosted tips of the San Francisco Peaks. Monsoon rains have wreaked havoc on the valley below, but each battle has proven a baptism. Head heavy, eyes rolling back to a mind you place in question, you concentrate on something you have not focused on in a long time: Inhale. You are going home: Exhale. You are going home: Home.

The End

ABOUT THE AUTHOR

NATHAN DOUGLAS HANSEN began his writing career in the Southwest, working as a feature writer and columnist for regional newspapers and magazines before attending Antioch University Los Angeles where he received his MFA. After university, Hansen became a literature instructor at a boarding school for at-risk youth and has since continued writing a column for various literary magazines. He is a veteran of the U.S. Army and lives in Sedona, Arizona.

Made in the USA
Middletown, DE
05 January 2016